Praise for

ASHA & THE SPIRIT BIRD

Winner of the Costa Children's Book Award 2019
Winner of the Times Children's Fiction Competition 2017
Chosen as one of the Guardian's best children's books of 2019
Shortlisted for the Waterstones Children's Book Prize 2020

'This book is such a light-filled, huge-hearted delight of an adventure.'
KATHERINE RUNDELL

'A beautifully evocative adventure, complete with prowling tigers
and mystical vultures, that follows a young girl's journey
through the Himalayas to find her father.'
ABI ELPHINSTONE

'This jewel of a book, suffused with colour, warmth, hope and, of course,
edge-of-your-seat adventure, is the perfect holiday read.
Every school should have a copy.'
LAUREN ST JOHN

'High stakes set against a vividly evoked setting, steeped in wild mysticism.
I was swept along by Asha's story from the first page.'
SARAH DRIVER

'An evocative debut novel . . . satisfyingly classic in feel.'
THE GUARDIAN

'. . . a heartfelt and mystical children's adventure story.'
THE TELEGRAPH

'. . . weaves themes of faith, friendship and greed into a vibrant
adventure with a rich seam of magic realism.'
THE BOOKSELLER

'[A] warm, comforting story . . . the final ending
is as perfect as any fairy tale.'

A MESSAGE FROM CHICKEN HOUSE

I love stories of wild islands, survival and *especially* magical animals – and this beautiful novel has all three! Aarti's adventure guides her towards secrets, legends and beliefs that will change her life for ever. No wonder this is Jasbinder Bilan's most astonishing story so far! It's magical and mystical – but also real, exciting and full of wisdom. Take this journey with Aarti and I promise you'll never forget it.

BARRY CUNNINGHAM
Publisher
Chicken House

JASBINDER BILAN

AARTI & THE BLUE GODS

Chicken House

2 Palmer Street, Frome, Somerset BA11 1DS
www.chickenhousebooks.com

Text © Jasbinder Bilan 2021
Cover illustration © Margaux Carpentier 2021

First published in Great Britain in 2021
Chicken House
2 Palmer Street
Frome, Somerset BA11 1DS
United Kingdom
www.chickenhousebooks.com

Chicken House/Scholastic Ireland, 89E Lagan Road, Dublin Industrial Estate,
Glasnevin, Dublin D11 HP5F, Republic of Ireland.

Cover and interior design by Steve Wells
Cover and interior illustrations by Margaux Carpentier
Map illustration © Alexis Snell 2021
Typeset by Dorchester Typesetting Group Ltd
Printed and bound in Great Britain by CPI Group (UK) Ltd, Croydon CR0 4YY

FSC
www.fsc.org
MIX
Paper from
responsible sources
FSC® C020471

1 3 5 7 9 10 8 6 4 2

British Library Cataloguing in Publication data available.

PB ISBN 978-1-913322-59-5
eISBN 978-1-913696-29-0

For Ian, Gem and Satchen –
with love always X

FOREST

THE GARDEN

STANDING
STONES

WALNUT
TREE

BEACH

THE OLD ABBEY

LOBSTER
POTS

AARTI'S
ISLAND

The clearest way into the Universe
is through a forest wilderness.

JOHN MUIR, *JOHN OF THE MOUNTAINS:*
THE UNPUBLISHED JOURNALS OF JOHN MUIR

Winter

If Aarti could fly, she wouldn't hang around here, she'd spread her wings and keep going until she landed somewhere else. Somewhere she felt she belonged and where she could find someone who loved her. She huffed cold breath on her numb fingers to warm them and watched the ladybirds as they gathered at the corners of the window.

'Aaaarti!' Aunt's voice tinkled up the stairs. 'It's nearly supper time – come down!'

Aarti scooped the red-and-black speckled ladybirds into her little tin, inched the mildewed window open a fraction and tipped the insects out into the deep winter evening.

The ladybirds flipped open their tiny wings and whizzed away. But Aarti knew that it didn't make any difference. However many times she did this, they always flew right back in. And, when she noticed them, Aunt Amalie would pop each one and crack its little shell. It made tears prick at Aarti's eyes every time.

'I'm making potato cakes,' came Aunt's voice again. 'Your favourites.'

Whenever Aunt called her name, Aarti heard another name flitting in the back of her mind – but it would never come to the front where she might catch it.

'Coming, Aunt!' she called.

She turned from the window, breathed down the butterflies that fluttered around her stomach and padded across the wooden floor of her bedroom. On the landing, she skirted round the metal bucket catching cold splashes of rainwater from the ceiling.

She walked past the dark door that Aunt always kept locked and that Aarti had never seen inside, along the corridor, past Aunt's room with its thick rug unfurled across the floorboards, and paused at the top of the stairs.

Peering down the curling bannister she saw her aunt standing at the very bottom, her bouncy blond curls tamed back into a bun, her cheeks rosy red from the fire. Aunt wore a grey tunic that came past her knees, over thick woollen trousers.

'There you are,' Aunt said, smiling. She was in a

good mood this evening. When Aunt was in a good mood it made Aarti nervous. She wasn't sure what she might do next. 'Come along, there's time for some reading before supper.'

Aarti tried to smile back. She owed Aunt so much and wanted to make her proud – it was just that sometimes she didn't know how to do it.

She made her way down the smooth wooden steps. The familiar homely smell wafted towards her from the range: fish guts from their morning catch mingled with the tang of woodsmoke. There was a darkened arched window at one end of the large hall and threadbare rugs scattered across the stone floor. Shelves lined the walls, heaving with books of all sizes.

Aunt was now sitting at a rustic table with a thick book spread open before her. The warmth from the crackling fire pumped blood to Aarti's cheeks and to the tip of her frozen nose. She felt herself relax a little.

Using a thick cloth to protect her hands, Aarti swung open the small metal door on the wood-burning range and checked the fire would last until morning. The logs smouldered orange and hissed when she added an extra piece of wood.

'Good girl, Aarti – we must never let the fire go out.'

'Yes, Aunt.' She smiled and felt her heart skip, allowed herself a beat of satisfaction. She shuffled on to the bench beside Aunt.

Aunt pointed to the words in the book with her pale finger, one by one, and as usual Aarti read out the words as clearly and as loudly as a hymn, just as Aunt had taught her.

> *Tyger Tyger, burning bright,*
> *In the forests of the night;*
> *What immortal hand or eye,*
> *Could frame thy fearful symmetry?'*

When Aarti had finished the verse, Aunt Amalie moved across to the griddle hanging above the fire and flipped the potato cakes. 'These will help you to have a good night's sleep, my dear,' she said, as she dabbed on some sheep's butter that made the cakes sizzle and sing. 'Isn't Aunt Amalie good? Making these for you? Your favourites.'

Aarti studied Aunt's face carefully, checking for the signs as she had learnt to do. 'Thank you, Aunt.'

'Fetch the honey from the store, would you, dear?'

Aarti heaved open the door beside the range and entered the dark storeroom with its earthy, sweet scent and shelves crammed with jars of preserves, honey from the beehives, dried herbs and mushrooms gathered through the year. The sheep gave them milk and butter, and meat that they dried for winter, packages of it carefully preserved and wrapped. On the floor, slumped like sleeping old men, were huge sacks of salt, oats to sow once spring came, and fresh oats from last autumn's harvest. Aunt was clever and a good planner and she worked hard to organize the store so they had everything they ever needed.

She had explained it all to Aarti, how they had to look after everything carefully so they could survive here – and how just as Aunt's parents had taught *her* to live on the island, so she was teaching Aarti. It was hard work, yes, but also a place where *they* were in control and where Aarti would be safe from a world full of bad, cruel things.

And anyway, Aunt knew everything and Aarti only knew the island.

She lifted a jar of honey and closed the door behind her, setting the jar on the side. She sat down at the table, watching Aunt as she left the potato cakes for a minute longer and then scooped three on to a wooden plate and placed it in front of Aarti.

Aarti gripped the edge of the plate when Aunt turned her back. The last time Aunt had been nice to her, it had ended with Aarti having to sleep in the woodstore because Aunt said she didn't seem very grateful and maybe needed time to think. It had been one of the coldest nights of deep winter and Aarti would surely have frozen, but Chand snuggled in beside her and then it wasn't too bad. She knew Aunt couldn't help it, and she did rub her feet with comfrey balm after.

Aarti was jolted back to the present as Aunt sat down opposite her at the long table. 'Beautiful reading, Aarti.'

'Thank you, Aunt.' She nibbled on a potato cake.

'Isn't this cosy?' Aunt continued. 'Let it rain, but here we are warm and we are fed.' Her voice softened. 'There's a big bad world out there, Aarti – you're lucky to be safe here on our island. Nobody to bother us or tell us what to do.' Aunt reached out, touched Aarti's chin and turned her face towards her. 'There is so much heartache out there.' Her eyes glistened. 'People who say they love you but don't really mean it. It's a cruel world.' She released Aarti, who instantly bowed her head, staring at her plate. Aunt's intensity was a bad sign. 'Lucky for you I shelter you from it . . . but remember, don't ever trust a man or a boy, Aarti. *I* know their ways.'

Aarti glanced up and nodded like she always did during Aunt's frequent talks about people's cruelty.

Although she knew Aunt had lived in a world with other people once, it also confused her – because how could every single person in the whole world be bad?

'And one day, Aarti,' continued Aunt, 'this whole island will be yours.' Aunt moved closer and put an arm round Aarti's shoulder. 'You were once a poor orphan that nobody wanted, and now look at you. Heir to the most beautiful place in the world.'

Aarti had heard this story a hundred times – but Aunt always left out the things Aarti burnt to know. Her heart pattered. 'And what happened to my parents?' she blurted.

Aunt's voice turned cold. 'They died, Aarti. I've told you. Don't be ungrateful now.' Aunt's grey eyes began to spark and she tugged at the loose strands of hair that had escaped from her bun.

Aarti swallowed and watched Aunt as she pulled rhythmically at the loose hair, the muscle in her jaw rippling as lightly as a feather.

'I . . . I'm not ungrateful,' she started, keeping her voice gentle. 'You told me how most people only want to adopt babies, but how you wanted *me* – your niece – over any bawling babies because you wanted a little girl of your own. I . . . it's just . . .' But she didn't dare continue.

Aunt's jaw relaxed slightly. 'Now then,' she said, composing her face and securing the hair back into her bun. 'Did you have a good day, my petal?'

'Yes, Aunt,' said Aarti, swallowing a mouthful of sweet, soft potato cake.

'Here, have some more honey.' Aunt Amalie dipped a spoon into the jar and drizzled deep-amber liquid over the potato cakes on Aarti's plate. 'What a treat – and it's not even your birthday! This year you will be twelve, Aarti. Can you believe it? We'll plan a special day for you. A picnic on the beach and a present. You will have a present. Something I have saved for you for a long time.'

'Thank you, Aunt.' Aarti stared into the fire. She wanted to be excited but she knew how it worked. How one day Aunt would entice her with the most wonderful treats and the next day she would pick fault with every tiny thing that Aarti did. Sometimes she would rage at her, throwing pans and plates on the floor, or make her do her ballet pliés for hours and hours on end.

Sometimes she would send her out in the deep snow and not allow her into the house until she'd performed some task. That was when she wandered the island with Chand. They would go to the safe place that Chand had shown her, the dry cave behind the waterfall in a hidden glade in the woods where she would make a bed of leaves for them both.

'What are you thinking, little one?' asked Aunt, tipping Aarti's chin and forcing her to look into her eyes again. Aunt's were a cold grey.

'N . . . nothing,' replied Aarti, her stomach clenching as she thought of what might happen if Aunt discovered her secrets.

Aunt held her chin. 'Such a beauty,' she whispered. 'An Indian princess living in the Scottish wilds.' She let go.

Aarti never understood what Aunt meant by this. It was one of the many things she said that didn't make any sense.

O nce Aunt Amalie was snoring by the fire, Aarti crept upstairs and fell into the creaking bed.

Spiders spun their cobwebs around her and cocooned Aarti as she tumbled into a heavy sleep.

The dream found its way to her, twisting and turning in the corners of her mind. It was a dream of a far-off place where the warm sun was shining and she was playing in a flower-filled garden. She picked a flower and it smelt so sweet. She walked through the garden and found a smiling woman with long dark hair who held out her arms. Aarti jumped into them. All her tiredness melted away as she snuggled in deep.

Drip, drip. Drops of cold rainwater landed on Aarti's head and woke her up. She opened her eyes to a small patch of dark sky and silver light from a full moon that poked into her room. She jumped on to the floor and dragged her bed away from the new hole in the roof, her breath puffing out into the freezing air, barely able to feel her numb toes. She bundled herself back under the blankets, drew her knees to her chest and watched the raindrops make a pool of water on the worn wooden floor, listening to the wind whistle.

She stayed like this, still thinking about the place in her dream, feeling the softness of the woman's hair, the touch of her arms around Aarti's. But every time she tried to look up at the woman's face, she always woke and found herself back here on this wild island where the only two people were Aunt and Aarti. Perhaps the woman was her mother, she thought – before she died. And the thought of what she had lost, even though she could barely dream it, made her so sad.

After a while, she stepped across the cold floor to the wall, lit the candle stub she kept there and traced the outline of the map she had drawn on the crumbling plaster. As she had grown older and explored the further reaches of the island, she had added new sections: the forest behind the house, the spot where the mushrooms grew in autumn, the hidden valley with the roaring waterfall, and the mountain with icy pools high up for swimming. Cliffs where Aunt sent her to collect eagle eggs, but Aarti never brought any back, because she couldn't bear to steal the chicks that were growing inside. And the standing stones above the harbour, a sign that once there had been more people here. Aarti took a piece of charcoal and drew another hole in the roof of their house, the half-ruined old abbey.

Even though it was still dark, Aarti heard Aunt Amalie's voice again and this time it didn't tinkle up the stairs but thundered. 'It's fishing time!'

Aarti knew there was no point in protesting. She blew out the candle, reached for the fishing rod that was stowed beside the wardrobe, put on an extra layer of socks and a jumper and bumbled down the stairs.

Aunt held the front door ajar while Aarti scrambled towards her, loaded with nets and the rod. Aarti paused a moment, unhooked an oversized waterproof from the rack and put it on. The muddy coat skimmed the floor and Aarti laid down the fishing things while she folded back the sleeves, her delicate hands poking from the ends.

'That's it, Aarti, wrap up. You get food for the day while I'll get fixing the leaky roof. It's teamwork.'

The wind smacked against her as soon as she stepped into the cold night, but Aarti held firm to the rods and nets, gripping them tightly.

'Be sure to check all the lobster pots,' shouted Aunt over the raging weather. 'All those years I had to look after you when you were small! Now that you're big enough, it's your turn to pay me back.'

The door slammed loudly behind her.

Once outside, Aarti breathed out and filled her lungs with fresh, salty air. She heard the wind ripple through the forest, which stretched all the way behind the house to the other side of the island.

As she walked away from the house, the rain started to weaken and the moon peeked out from between the clouds, lighting the path – though she'd walked it in the dark a hundred times. After glancing over her shoulder to check she was far enough from the house, she whistled. In less than a heartbeat, Chand appeared beside her like magic. He rubbed against her leg and Aarti put down the fishing tools, bending low to stroke his red fur, and planted a kiss on the white-moon shape on his forehead.

The name 'Chand' had come to her as soon as she'd seen the crescent shape, though she wasn't sure why. His pointed ears, tipped ice white, pricked, and even in the darkness his eyes sparkled as he swept the cold air with the brush of his tail. Sometimes Aarti wondered if he had been sent by some magic to light up her never-ending days and nights.

'If it weren't for you, dear Chand,' said Aarti, searching his dark eyes, flecked with amber, 'I don't know what I'd do.'

Chand had been on the island for as long as she could remember, but last autumn, he had disappeared for a few days and she'd found him whimpering, buried under a pile of crisp leaves, close to the house. His paw was hurt and Aarti had saved food from her own plate and nursed him until he was strong enough to run again. Now, he always stayed close.

He nuzzled into Aarti's palm and she brought out the moss-green pumpkin seeds she'd saved for him. She harvested them from the giant pumpkins they grew and dried them out in the warm autumn sun. 'There you are. My very own magical fox.'

She picked up the fishing rod again and Chand trotted beside her until they were down by the natural harbour, with its swooping curved beach and the black sea, frantic in the moonlight. The fierce wind churned up the waves and they crashed on to the pale beach. Aarti yanked up the hood on her coat, pushing her long plait so it slipped down her back.

First, she went to the rocks on the far side of the beach and checked the lobster pots for any signs of a catch. She balanced easily on the slippery rocks, but the wind tugged at her hood and snapped it back as she peered into the pots they'd made from bendy hazel branches.

Only one small crab.

Chand sniffed the air as Aarti scooped some salt water into her bucket and dropped the crab in.

Next, she set up the fishing rods with their bait of worms and waited for the fish to bite. Aarti shivered and yawned as she stood on the rocks, wishing she'd managed to sleep for longer. Aunt said the best fish came out at night, so she woke her up twice a week and sent her night-fishing. But even though it was so cold that Aarti could barely feel her fingers and her feet were so numb they felt like small blocks of ice, she was happiest away from Aunt's changeable temper. She hadn't always been this bad. Lately, she'd been getting worse.

As if he guessed what Aarti was thinking, Chand came closer and snuggled against her leg, making a mewling sound that rose like a night song into the air and carried on the wind across the sea.

'I wonder what's out there?' said Aarti, staring into the night. 'Do you think there's anyone else anywhere at all? Or is it just me and Aunt and you, Chand, on our little island?'

Aarti felt her heart tighten at the thought and a strange feeling of missing someone that she couldn't quite remember. As she gripped the fishing rod tighter, she pictured her fingers curled around another hand. Not Aunt's. The feeling was faint but firm and it brought with it an unexpected tear, which slid down her cheek. Why were these images rising up recently, in dreams and unexpected moments? Could they really be memories?

Aarti fixed the rod between the rocks and crouched down to Chand who moved closer, warming Aarti with his thick fur. She breathed in his scent of wilderness and the tip of her nose unfroze a little. Chand looked up into Aarti's face, and with his velvet tongue licked the salty tears away.

3

A few hours later, the moon shone into the bucket, lighting up the deep-green crab scrabbling around in the water and the shimmering scales on the fish that Aarti had caught.

Aunt was bound to be pleased by her night's work, but even as she formed this thought it smudged out faster than a setting sun, because Aarti knew that Aunt Amalie would never be truly happy, ever. Why was it so hard to please her these days?

She gathered her things and started back to the house, the water slapping the sides of the bucket and the crab making splashing, snapping sounds.

With Chand by her side Aarti felt strong. She decided she wouldn't let Aunt Amalie make her sad today, however mean she was. She kept this thought clear in her head as they got closer to home.

The dishevelled stone house appeared suddenly

over the next hill. It was a long building with arched leaded windows on the ground floor and smaller rectangular ones above, like a small church with its peaked roof. It was, Aarti thought, like a surprise in the landscape.

The patched-up roof shone under the light of the moon and bats circled the chimney stacks, swooping in and out of the holes.

The moon cast shadows ahead and the wind carried a mournful tune. It whistled through the woods behind the house with notes that sounded like a musical instrument and made Aarti stop and listen. It was like the universe was speaking to her, and three notes lilted and hung over the roof of the house, as if it knew that Aarti was returning to a place empty of love, but she wasn't forgotten.

Aarti kissed Chand goodnight and he stayed, like he always did, by the foot of the great walnut tree, until she disappeared back into the house.

She closed the door as softly as she could, hoping that Aunt Amalie wouldn't hear so she could slip upstairs without being noticed and go back to bed.

But as soon as Aarti stepped into the house Aunt whirled upon her. 'So?' she boomed. 'Did you do well with your fishing trip? Will we feast or will we starve?'

Aarti slopped the bucket on to the floor by way of an answer and rubbed her numb hands together. In the big hall the fire was burning in the hearth, as it always was.

'May I warm myself by the fire?' asked Aarti. 'It's such a bitter night.'

Aunt Amalie took her hands and examined them. 'No frostbite yet . . . you must toughen up. Work first, Aarti, and then warming by the fire.'

Aarti remembered her promise to herself: she wasn't going to let Aunt make her sad. She drew herself up, her voice gentle but firm. 'But Aunt, I'm tired and cold and soaked through. The wind tonight was so fierce it whipped the waves high against the shore.' She showed Aunt her soaking clothes where the water had trickled under the raincoat. 'Can't I dry off first? I can do my chores right after.'

'Poor mite,' said Aunt, stepping closer. She gripped Aarti's cheek between her thick finger and thumb and pinched tightly.

'Ow!' Aarti pulled backwards, her cheek smarting. She gazed at Aunt in horror – she'd never done that before.

Something like regret flickered in Aunt's eyes – but the hard grey gleam returned all too quickly. 'There, there. It wasn't so hard, Aarti! Now, stop making a fuss. Just an affectionate little touch. Run along now, the pot is boiling – did you fetch any crab?' She peered into the bucket. 'Only a little one? How are we to survive? Try harder, Aarti – what a disappointment.' Her face clouded over and she pinched her lips together.

Aarti struggled to see how it was her fault that the basket had only caught one crab, but she bit her tongue. 'I'll pop it in the pot,' she said instead, hoping to distract Aunt. 'And we can salt the fish for another day.'

'Go on then,' said Aunt grumpily. 'I'm going back to bed.'

Aarti swallowed. She wouldn't let Aunt get the better of her. She rubbed her cheek and thought of Chand sitting by the walnut tree, staying with her whenever she went out, and the strange music she'd heard. The notes had stirred her heart and filled her mind with racing thoughts, helping her to stay strong.

In the morning the wind was still blustering about the house, rattling at the small window in Aarti's room and piping through the gaps. But at least the hole in the roof was patched and the damp spot on the floor had dried up.

Aarti stepped lightly across her room to a pile of books she'd brought from the shelves in the hall. She heaved some into her arms and snuggled back into her warm bed. It was one of the things that Aunt didn't seem to mind. She thought reading and learning were good and that you could find out anything from books. And when Aunt slept in late, it meant that Aarti could lose herself in stories.

A pale winter sun seeped across the floor, lighting up the open page on Aarti's lap. This was one of her favourite books. It was all about Hindu gods and goddesses. Each page had a beautiful painting of an incredible creature that seemed to be human but also strange. There was one page where the god had an elephant's head but a man's body, another where the fierce goddess Durga rode a lion and had ten arms, each holding a weapon to defeat her enemies.

But the section that Aarti loved more than any other was the one all about the god Krishna. He looked so happy in the painting, surrounded by the most beautiful white cows.

Aarti traced her finger across his face, fascinated by the deep-blue colour of his skin. Light from the window brightened the room, bathing Krishna in a golden glow, shining on the flute he wore around his neck, and Aarti felt a spark of hope.

There was a poem in the book that Aarti didn't fully understand but loved. When she read it she felt less alone. It talked about the god Krishna being the centre of everything – the seas, mountains, skies and all the animals. When she walked the island, she imagined how it would feel to be like him, to *be* the island itself.

When the sun was higher, she closed the book and tucked it under her pillow, made her bed and quietly left her room.

On the landing, she saw Aunt's door was firmly closed. Perhaps it would be one of those days when she slept all day. She tapped lightly on the door. 'Aunt, are you OK?'

'I'm tired, Aarti,' came the muffled voice from the other side. 'Just tired – that's all.'

'I'll bring you some tea later, shall I?'

Aunt didn't reply.

Aarti walked past the locked door. When she was younger she had never thought much about it, but for the last year she had grown more and more curious, wondering what was behind the door that needed to be locked away, and she began to think about the key and where Aunt might have put it.

She tiptoed down the stairs and into the big hall. The fire was still glowing. She poked it with the metal rod and put some logs on. The grey ash parted and she blew at the flickering flames, bringing them back to life. Next she creaked open the door on the range and checked the fire, making sure it too was stoked up for the day.

She found a mug of warm tea that Aunt had left for her on the range and smiled. Sometimes it was hard to remember that Aunt loved her – but she did, in her way. She took the mug to a stool beside the fire and wrapped her hands around it, sipping the sweet herbal tea slowly. Afterwards, she heated up a potato cake from the night before and ate it up, listening all the time for the sound of Aunt's footsteps that she knew might clatter down at any moment.

But Aunt didn't come down and there was no noise from the room above, so Aarti got on with her chores. She collected eggs from the chickens, checked on the sheep in the field to the side of the house, dug up a cabbage from the garden ready for soup later and set aside the crab from the night before. All the while she thought more and more about what was behind the locked door. She felt guilty – Aunt had saved her when nobody else wanted her, and brought her to this place she loved so much. She should count herself lucky that they had the island – which would one day belong to Aarti, Aunt had promised.

But if Aunt was telling the whole truth, what was she hiding in the locked room? And what about the dreams Aarti had been having, the unexpected visions which felt a lot like buried memories?

As Aarti went back inside, she had a sudden idea: she would take her Krishna book to the special place that Chand had led her to. It was a place that Aunt didn't know about, a dry cave behind the waterfall, deep in the woods. She had made a sort of shrine there, just like they had in the book. It was somewhere completely her own, where she felt calm and could make wishes. When she was there, perhaps she could send a wish out into the world – a wish for truth.

She crept back to her room and silently bundled the book in a blanket. She listened a moment outside Aunt's bedroom door – silence – before hurrying downstairs, shoving on her woollen hat and coat and placing the book carefully in the rucksack. The door closed soft as a murmur. Bubbles of happiness fizzed in Aarti's stomach. She was out!

The sun was bright in the pale blue sky and Aarti hurried to the walnut tree where Chand sat patiently waiting, his head in the air, a warm ray of hope and love beneath the bare branches.

'Let's go to our special place, Chand.'

Aarti kissed him on the forehead, and together they headed into the forest, tripping along under the stark branches, the ground thickly layered with dried leaves. She listened for the musical notes she'd heard the evening before, but the wind had dropped and there was only the crunch of her feet as they swept across the forest floor.

She walked quickly, in case Aunt had heard her leave, afraid that she'd call her back. She broke into a run. Chand rustled along the soft ground beside her and they hurried between the trees, brightness shimmering through the dark branches and bathing Aarti and Chand in winter sun.

Far from the house, Aarti slipped the hat into her pocket, tugged her plait loose and let the dark hair tumble down her back. They found the wide river that started in the mountains and rushed over rocks, slowing as it meandered through the forest. They rested on the damp bank and watched the water flowing slick as silver over the grey, mottled stones.

Chand leapt on to Aarti's lap and she buried her face in his flame-coloured fur. He made a soulful bark and stared into Aarti's eyes, like he was reaching for the hurt and hoping to make it better. And he always did.

'What's going to happen, Chand?' asked Aarti. 'I want to find out the whole truth about my past – but Aunt hardly tells me a thing. If anything, it seems like she's hiding something. Do *you* think I should send out a wish for answers? From our special place –

our shrine?' She'd read the word in the book of blue gods.

Chand stared more fiercely into her eyes. Aarti wasn't sure if she was just imagining things, but whenever she spoke to Chand about her troubles, or asked him a question, he always looked more deeply, as if he really understood what she was saying.

Suddenly he jumped on to the bank and began running about, tugging at Aarti's coat in the direction of the shrine, as if wanting her to chase him.

'OK,' she giggled. 'I'll take that as a yes!' And she ran after him.

They followed the rushing river as it snaked its way through the peat-scented forest, dipping and rising over rocks frosted with silver lichens. Aarti slowed to a walk as the ground started to steepen and her legs grew tired. She paused at the hollow tree, climbed up and pushed her hand into the dry space inside, bringing out the moss package she'd left there last time, filled with dried berries and mushrooms. She slipped the treats into her pocket. 'We'll share these later,' she explained to Chand, who was panting as he waited for her to follow.

Finally, near the river's source, Chand and Aarti squeezed through a narrow opening made between two huge boulders – the entrance to their secret place. The gap was too small for Aunt, which perhaps was why she had never found it . . . and she never had a special fox friend to show her the way. Here, a large pool of forest-green water gleamed brightly and bubbled where the waterfall cascaded down.

Aarti led the way as she stepped carefully along the ledge that led behind the roaring waterfall, the scent of forest water filling her nose, and ducked into the dry cave beyond. Chand slipped in behind her.

Despite the roar of the waterfall, Aarti immediately felt safe and calm here – she loved this place Chand had found for her. At the back of the cave a natural stone shelf jutted from a wall covered in bright green moss.

The shelf was her shrine. Aarti rearranged the items she'd already placed there: blue stones collected from the beach, ridged shells as pale as bone, and golden leaves as big as her hand. Once she'd cleared a space, she unwrapped the Krishna book and set it on the shelf, laying the blanket beneath it.

Aarti blinked and took a deep breath, placing her palm on the book as sunlight pierced through the waterfall and shone into the cave. She felt Chand sit down at her side. She searched her mind and tried to go back to the garden of her dreams – maybe she could make the memories stronger, will them to come forward and show themselves to her. She opened the book at the poem she loved and read it aloud:

'*I am the pure fragrance in earth and brightness of fire . . .*'

As she spoke the words, she felt like she was waking something up, calling out to something she didn't understand but that made her feel like she mattered.

'Please,' she said softly. 'I just want to know the truth about who I am.'

After a few moments, the light beam shifted and the cave was thrown into shadow. Aarti lowered her hand from the book. The moment was over. Chand nudged at her pocket, whining slightly.

'OK, OK,' she said, smiling.

They sat together by the entrance, spray from the waterfall wetting Aarti's lashes as she fished into her pocket. She offered her palm to Chand and he delicately picked a few berries.

'I have to find the key to the locked room,' murmured Aarti, eyes fixed on the falling water. 'When I was younger I didn't mind not knowing. Aunt's kept me safe all this time, and I do trust her. If she's hiding anything, it's probably to keep me safe, don't you think?' She glanced over at Chand. He gazed up at her, his eyes intent. 'But she doesn't understand. I get flashes of shadowy people and places that I can't explain and I have to know more. Who are they, Chand? Who were my parents? Why is the room locked? What's in there – what is she protecting me from?' She sighed. 'Sorry, Chand. I know you'd help me if you could. But I think I'll have to help myself.'

Aarti knew she shouldn't stay out too late. It would soon begin to get cold, Aunt would probably have woken up by now, and even though she didn't want to, she knew they ought to be getting back. 'Come on, Chand,' she whispered, wrapping the blanket carefully around her book to protect it, but leaving it on the shelf – it felt right to keep it here.

Outside the cave, Aarti balanced on the edge of the pool and stared at the reflection in the water. Who was this girl? Her sharp-featured face, ruddy cheeks and wild, tangled hair suddenly felt so unfamiliar.

As she walked home, Chand trotting at her side, Aarti felt different, as if the water had shown her a new version of herself. She couldn't shake the sense that she had new power, if only she could capture it.

On the home straight, the sky turned from blue to purple over the sea, the winter sun from pale amber to deep red. Aarti watched the clouds as they shifted shape. Then, her breath caught and she stopped.

'Look, Chand!' she said, pointing.

Krishna floated up there in the clouds, beaming down at her from high above, his fingers pressed to a flute. She recalled the line again from the poem and shouted it loudly to the blue Krishna in the sky who hovered over her:

'I am the pure fragrance in earth and brightness of fire!'

She felt her cheeks blaze with heat even though the wind was cool and she watched as the image of Krishna moved over the whole sky, turning wispy and ragged though his face, visible until the last, carried on smiling down at her. Faintly, above the sound of the sea came the three notes she had heard in the forest before, but this time it was as if they were all around her, coming from all directions.

Aarti stood up and climbed on to a rock, stared out across the sea, at the whole of the island. She could see the lethal cliffs way away on the far side, the tops of the trees of the deep forest, the soft curve of the white beach beside the harbour where she went fishing, and the chimney stacks of the old abbey.

'Did you hear Krishna's flute too, Chand?'

He twitched his ears.

She tidied her hair and plaited it quickly, pulling her hat more firmly on her head. Whatever she'd seen and heard, it was getting late – she really had to get home.

By the time they arrived at the walnut tree, day had disappeared like the blink of an eye and night was creeping close once more. Aarti gazed up one last time into the deep-indigo sky, at the stars that now flashed silver. Chand gave a small yelp and padded towards the sleek bodies of three more foxes. He gave Aarti a goodbye look before running towards them.

Aarti felt her heart ache as she turned towards the silent house, alone.

On days when Aunt stayed in bed she could be even more unpredictable, and Aarti didn't know if she would hug her and lavish her in kindness – or be cross that she'd left her alone all day. She took a deep breath.

As soon as she clicked open the front door, Aunt's fierce face appeared in front of her, waiting in the doorway.

5

'Where have you been?' Aunt cried. 'I was distraught.'

Aunt's hair had escaped from its usual bun and it sprang wildly about her face. Her eyes were rimmed red and she hadn't dressed. The breeze whooshed through the open door and flapped her flowered gown around her ankles.

Aarti's hands trembled as she shut the door and hung her hat and coat on the peg, her stomach churning at what might happen next.

'I went for a walk,' she said calmly.

Aunt marched towards Aarti and grabbed her tightly by the wrists. 'I was waiting and waiting.'

'Aunt, that hurts.' Aunt loosened her grip slightly. Aarti tried to pull away but Aunt didn't let her. 'You were still sleeping,' she continued. 'I thought it would be better if I went out for a while – quieter for you. So you could rest. But I'm here now.' Her eyes stung as she lowered her gaze to the flagstones.

Eventually Aunt released Aarti, the strange, guilty expression flashing across her face before she composed herself once again, tucking the loose hair neatly into her bun.

Aarti studied Aunt carefully from under her lashes. Over the years, Aarti had learnt that she had to be vigilant, one step ahead of Aunt's moods. She could never let her guard down . . . and that was exhausting. Especially now they were getting harder and harder to predict.

'Let's make supper,' said Aunt, 'and after that you need to do your ballet. We might be on an island at the ends of the earth, Aarti, but don't let anyone say that I didn't think about your education.' She drew herself up, her voice gathering confidence. 'I want to give you all the best chances in life, embrace you with art and culture, just like my parents did for me.'

Aarti smiled encouragingly. 'Great! By the way, I collected eggs this morning, five – not too bad. We could have them for supper?'

Aunt smiled back. 'Let's go then. We can cook together.' She led Aarti into the hall and grabbed an onion from the string that hung from a beam in the ceiling. She began chopping the onion furiously.

Aarti lifted the eggs carefully from the store and cracked them into a dish, beating them together with a fork before handing them to Aunt, who had started to sing. Her shoulders relaxed slightly. The danger wasn't over yet, but it looked like Aarti had managed to avoid the worst of Aunt's temper.

'Did you find the tea I left for you on the stove?' Aunt took the eggs and splashed them into the heavy pan once the onions were golden brown. 'I didn't feel too well this morning, but I thought about you, Aarti. I do think about you.'

'Yes, thank you, Aunt.' She knew that there were days when Aunt couldn't face the simplest of tasks and it was kind of her to leave the tea.

Aunt smiled and continued to cook the eggs. 'You must have been cold out there today.'

'The sun was out,' said Aarti, 'and the sky was blue. It was a beautiful day.'

'And I missed it.' Aunt's lip wobbled just slightly.

'It might be nice again tomorrow. Maybe we can go for a walk together.' A rumble of thunder sounded outside and Aarti winced. She sensed which way the evening might go and she tried hard to distract Aunt from dwelling on her disappointment. 'Are the eggs ready? Eating will make you feel better, Aunt.'

They sat side by side on the bench and ate their supper by the light of the orange flames from the fire, night-time sending shadows spinning across the walls. Outside, a storm had begun to crash against the roof and rain fell in torrents above them.

'Lucky I managed to repair those leaks,' said Aunt, when their plates were nearly clean. 'The tiles have been on the roof since I was a little girl like you, but they'll still be good for another hundred years.'

'Did you always live here?' Aarti risked asking a question. Sometimes Aunt didn't mind answering; at other times she shut it down quick as a clap. This was one of those times.

'Ballet practice,' Aunt announced, as she swept away Aarti's plate. 'Chop chop. Go get changed.' She clattered the dishes into the sink and pulled a violin from under the bench.

Aarti's stomach sank but she hurried upstairs and pulled on her dark plum-coloured tutu with its stretchy waist and the tights that Aunt had cut the feet off when she complained that they were too short. She ran back down barefoot.

'Ah . . . my little ballerina.' Aunt peered at Aarti's feet. 'Ballet slippers?'

'They're too small, Aunt,' Aarti said.

'Ballerinas must suffer for their art, what's a little

pinching? Go get them on.'

Aarti ran back up the stairs and pushed her feet into the slippers, listening to the sound of Aunt tuning her instrument. The slippers were the same ones she'd always had and her toes curled painfully against the worn leather at the end. She gritted her teeth and hobbled back to the hall where Aunt stood ready by the fire, poised with the violin tucked beneath her chin.

'Ready?' Aunt began to play and Aarti started her warm-up under Aunt's instructions, although she didn't need her to tell her what to do. She knew the routine and could have run through it in her sleep. It was the number of jumps and pliés that were gruelling as Aunt counted and played.

The pinching of the slippers and the thumping of her curled toes against the stone floor brought tears to Aarti's eyes, but she tried to focus on the music. The violin filled the hall with a beautiful, soulful sound until finally Aunt allowed her to take off the slippers and do free dancing around the room.

Relief filled Aarti's body – the worst was over. She twirled and jumped while Aunt, eyes firmly closed, was totally wrapped up in the music until finally, after an hour or more, the music stopped and Aarti was allowed to rest.

She slumped next to the fire, her arms and legs aching, her breath beating out of her. Aunt threw herself on the bench, her face pale despite the heat in the room, her cheeks damp. After the ballet sessions they were always both exhausted. It was as though Aunt had relived all the pain of her life and flung it out into her playing. It lined her brow and shone from her eyes.

'Go to bed, Aarti.' Aunt's voice was barely a whisper and Aarti slipped from the room, leaving Aunt collapsed over the table, her head resting on her arms.

As Aarti hurried up the stairs, she passed the locked door on the landing and paused in front of it, grasped the doorknob and gave it a twist, but it stayed shut.

She knelt and pushed her head to the floor, then peered into the gap between the boards and the bottom of the door. She saw nothing but darkness.

A arti was woken by a gentle tapping on her door and then Aunt's face which peered around it, carrying a tray of breakfast things.

'Are you awake yet?' whispered Aunt. 'I'm sorry about yesterday.' She sat on the edge of Aarti's bed and sighed. 'But I'm going to make it up to you today.' Pale sunshine swept across the floorboards and on to the bed. 'Am I forgiven? I only want the best for you.'

Aarti sat up and Aunt plumped the pillows. 'I'm going to spoil you.' She handed Aarti a mug of tea and began cracking the boiled egg that sat in a cute little egg cup. 'Here.' She scooped the golden, runny yolk and slipped it into Aarti's mouth.

'Thank you, Aunt.' Aarti swallowed it down with a glug of tea and she snuggled against Aunt, letting her stroke her hair. This was how it had been when she was younger – she wished Aunt was like this more often.

After the breakfast was eaten Aunt brought Aarti a jumper from her room. 'This was mine when I was your age. My mother, your granny, knitted it for me and it's yours now.'

Aarti pulled it on over her pyjamas and traced the swirly letter *A* knitted in red wool against the cream. She sniffed the sleeve – it had a herbal smell.

'I kept it wrapped in tissue paper with lengths of juniper to keep it fresh. A for Amalie and A for Aarti.'

'It's so cosy.' It really was. She hugged it close. 'I love it!'

'Come on, let's go to the beach.' There was a gleam of excitement in Aunt's eyes. 'I've got a surprise for you . . . but stay here until I call you. I want to get everything ready myself.' And off she swept, out of the room and down the stairs.

Aarti felt a buzz of excitement; maybe today would be a day when Aunt would be nice all day long. It didn't happen very often any more, but Aarti remembered a few times when she didn't flip at some point, when the whole day was one to be treasured, filled with warm memories that made Aarti under-stand Aunt more and made her feel that Aunt really cared about her like a proper mother.

Aarti got out of bed and looked at her reflection in the windowpane. She rolled up the sleeves of the jumper. It was a little long but apart from that it fitted well. It felt so special to have something that wasn't worn and she twirled in front of her image. She untied her plait and shook her hair loose.

Aunt's voice reached up the stairs. 'You can come down now, it's all ready!'

Aarti ran out to the stairs.

'Ahhh, look at you, darling . . .' Aunt was standing in the hall with the picnic basket all packed.

Aarti blushed. Why couldn't Aunt be like this more often?

'I've packed us a picnic. And the surprise.' She patted her pocket.

The day was another beautiful one, the sky a milky blue and the sun shining over the woods. Aarti hooked her arm through Aunt's and breathed deeply. 'Thank you.'

Aunt didn't say anything but she pulled Aarti a little closer, and together they made their way along the track which led to the beach. The sea was emerald green, clear and still, stretching away from the island. The grey-headed guillemots spread their white wings close to the sea's surface before disappearing under its slick cover in search of fish.

Aunt took a blanket from the bag and spread it out on the drier sand a little way from the water's edge. 'I'll collect rocks to make our firepit.'

'And I'll find dry firewood,' said Aarti. She climbed on to the bank above the beach and picked stray branches from under the trees, watching Aunt as she hauled rocks and made a circle with them. It had been so long since Aarti had felt what she was feeling right now, the swelling in her chest, but she guessed it was love. Aunt wasn't a bad person. Aarti still longed to know more about her own past – and Aunt's too – but deep down she knew that no matter what, Aunt really did love her too. She waved and Aunt stopped what she was doing, flashed her a big smile and sent her a huge wave back.

Aarti bundled the sticks into her outstretched arms and carried them down to the firepit. Aunt had already begun to build a wigwam with kindling she had in the bag, and then she knelt close with the flint and steel and pressed the coil of wood shavings into the space below the sticks.

'Well done, Aarti,' breathed Aunt, pushing back a lock of hair and tucking it behind her ear. She flashed the flint against the steel until it sparked orange and lit the shavings all at once, the flames leaping on to the kindling and starting the fire. 'We'll build it slowly,' she murmured. 'Pass me the wood a branch at a time.'

'Here.' Aarti enjoyed seeing Aunt doing practical things; it was when she seemed most happy, lost in creating something. She had once said it kept away the thoughts that swooped into her mind and crammed it with too much thinking, over and over.

'We make a good team . . . don't we, Aarti?'

'Yes,' Aarti replied, taking in a deep happy breath.

Aarti warmed herself by the fire while Aunt continued to pile the branches around the flames. She staked two special branches firmly on either side of the fire and balanced a kettle filled with water between them on a metal rod.

They made tea and sipped it in silence while watching the gentle waves frothing white in the distance. Aarti was lost in her thoughts. Since catching sight of her reflection by the waterfall she'd felt different, like she was changing – growing out of the skin she'd become so used to. She scanned the clouds for signs of Krishna, strained her ears for sounds of the flute. But she didn't see or hear anything.

Aunt turned to her. 'You're growing up . . . you were so tiny when I brought you here.'

Aarti's heart speeded up – was Aunt finally going

to tell her about her past?

Aunt dipped her fingers into her pocket and brought out a package, wrapped in a square of flowered fabric, and handed it to Aarti.

She swallowed and opened the package, Aunt's eyes studying her carefully. 'Oh . . . it's beautiful.' Aarti placed the brooch in her palm. It was in the shape of a seahorse, its clear gemstones sparkling in the sunlight.

'It belonged to my mother and she gave it to me. They're diamonds . . . the stones, I mean. I know you don't understand, but they're precious – worth a lot of money.'

Aarti crinkled her brow. 'It's so pretty.' She wrapped her arms tight around Aunt's waist, like she used to when she was little. 'I love it, thank you.'

Aunt smiled. 'Here.' She took it from Aarti's palm and pinned it to her jumper. 'Happy birthday, Aarti.'

'I . . . it's my *birthday*?'

'Sort of . . .' Her voice trailed off. 'It's around the time I adopted you.'

Aarti waited for Aunt to say more, her heart fluttered as she silently pleaded – but Aunt's mouth was clamped shut.

Disappointment crashed down. Aarti didn't know what to feel. It was so kind of Aunt to celebrate the day, but what had come before? She wanted to ask . . . but she pushed the thoughts to the back of her mind. Today was a good day; she didn't want to spoil it. 'Thank you,' she murmured.

'Let's toast hazelnuts,' Aunt said. She tipped a bag of nuts into a small frying pan and began shaking it over the flames. 'Life's not too bad on the island, is it, Aarti?'

'No . . . it isn't too bad,' she whispered.

Spring

7

The long winter days and nights passed as usual with chores, reading and dance practice. Whenever she could, Aarti slipped outside and explored the island with Chand. She imagined how it would be if there were other people on the island, like the characters in the books lining the shelves in the hall.

She would make up stories and tell them to Chand, who always appeared to listen intently, apparently enthralled. Her favourite stories were those in which she really was an Indian princess, just like Aunt had told her, and this island was her vast and beautiful kingdom.

One night in early spring, when everything was still shrouded in darkness and rain had been falling for days, Aarti was woken by clattering and banging, dragging and bumping. She pulled the covers tight over her head and bundled herself into a tense ball, trying to make herself invisible, as if she could magic herself away. She knew that if Aunt came in, she would tear off the blanket, filled with some dreaded idea, and Aarti would have to go along with it – whatever it was.

She listened for Aunt's footsteps all through the noisy night, but she didn't come into Aarti's room, and then suddenly, as a pale yellow sun seeped through the cobwebbed windows, the front door slammed and the house fell deathly quiet.

Aarti stayed still for a moment before pushing back the blanket and stepping on to the icy floor. She stood by the window and watched as Aunt tramped through the mud, a bulging rucksack on her back, walking away from the house. Aarti noticed the first fresh buds appearing on the trees and the chitter-chatter of birds as they swooped to collect twigs and straw for nests, and it made her feel hopeful.

She rushed out of the bedroom on to the landing. She was about to walk past the locked room, but stopped. Her nerves jangled as her eyes fell to the brass key that was dangling from the door.

Her heart thudded loudly in her chest as she took a deep breath, twisted the knob and creaked the door open. The room was dark and filled with shadowy piles of boxes, placed higgledy-piggledy on top of each other. Flicking a quick look over her shoulder, Aarti stepped inside the forbidden room.

Could this be the answer to her prayer for truth?

If Aunt came back and found her in here, she would definitely punish her, and the thought made Aarti's heart beat quicker against her ribs.

She wasn't sure what she was looking for, but she felt certain there must be something in here that would tell her about her past, give some answers to the hundreds of questions that stayed locked inside Aarti's head, the ones Aunt had refused to answer.

She knew she must be careful to leave everything exactly as it was so Aunt wouldn't suspect that she'd been here, and swiftly began peering inside the boxes without moving them. Aarti didn't see anything interesting, just yellowing papers filled with writing about the abbey and lists of materials bought. In her hurry, Aarti stumbled backwards, knocking a box over, and when she peered in, she found a metal tin with faded birds painted on it.

Inside the tin was a bundle of letters wrapped with a green ribbon.

Aarti pulled one out and in the bleak light began to read:

Dear Mummy

How long do I have to stay here? I don't like being away from you and Daddy. I have to sleep in a dorm with lots of other girls and all of them snore. I haven't made any friends like you said I would.

PLEEEEEEAAAASE MUMMY CAN I COME HOME?????

I promise I will be good and I won't lose my temper. I also miss Seasalt. Is he behaving? Is he missing me?

Love you lots and lots

Amalie XXXXXXXXXXXXXXX

Aarti untied the ribbon and flicked through the rest of the letters. They were all about missing Mummy and Daddy, about food at the school being horrible and about how Amalie couldn't wait for the holidays. Aarti felt a pang of sadness for Aunt that there was only one reply to all of her letters, and it only talked about how Amalie had to make the best of things and study hard if she wanted to do well.

Folding the letters neatly, Aarti tied the ribbon and put them back in the tin. Disappointment tugged at her heart. She couldn't find anything about herself and didn't dare spend too long here, in case

Aunt came back and found her in the middle of this room she clearly didn't want her to see. A noise outside made her jump. She had to get out quickly!

Aarti frantically scanned the room one last time and just as she was about to leave, she saw a pale-coloured clump discarded in the far corner, covered in cobwebs. She wasn't sure why but she hurried over and picked it up, shook off the dust and dirt and held it in her hands.

It was a toy rabbit with floppy ears that fell either side of its face. Aarti felt dizzy. She clasped it to her chest, leaning back against the wall. The feel of it, and even the smell beneath the dust, awakened a faint memory, something that Aarti couldn't explain or grasp hold of. But she knew this rabbit was hers.

She found the place under its arm and her fingers felt for the strangely familiar tag. Looking down at the carefully embroidered writing, she noticed how the red thread was dirtied from lying on the floor all these years. It read:

My name is Squidgy Rabbit –
if I'm lost please return to Lantern Hall,
Blackberry Lane, Nottinghamshire

Aarti backed out of the room unsteadily, holding the toy in her hand. She left the key hanging in the lock, just as she had found it, pulled the door closed and stumbled into her bedroom.

It was as if she were in a dream. At first she sat up in bed still as a statue, allowing the whirlwind of thoughts to cascade into her mind. As she drew her toy closer she felt its head turn damp. Even then she was confused. Her eyes welled up and tears sneaked out and she couldn't make them stop. As if she were watching herself from above, she observed her body shaking, saw each teardrop reflect the early-morning light.

Somebody had given her this toy; she knew it belonged to her and she knew the memories it held were hers – but why would Aunt leave it in the locked room? As she closed her eyes, a shadowy image flashed and pulled her back: Aunt's hand wrapped firmly around her own . . .

A feeling caught tight in her throat. She was scared. Fresh tears dropped on her cheeks and she slumped against the pillow.

None of this proved much, but maybe Aunt was covering something up. Aarti unpinned the seahorse brooch from her jumper and fastened it to Squidgy Rabbit's chest. She held him tightly, her heart thumping against his fur, and drifted into a numb sleep.

8

Aarti was woken by the loud bang of the front door and footsteps thudding up the stairs. They paused on the landing and Aarti's stomach clenched at the thought of the key still dangling in the lock of the forbidden room next door. She quickly pushed her cuddly toy under the pillow and closed her eyes again before Aunt's windswept face appeared over the bed, looming towards her.

'Are you ill?'

Aarti blinked, crusts of tears still binding her lids closed. 'I . . . I don't feel well. I've been in bed all day.'

Aunt touched Aarti's red cheeks. 'Maybe you have a fever.' She narrowed her eyes. Aarti didn't flinch, but studied Aunt's pale grey irises with their circle of gold rimming the dark pupils. Was she hiding something?

Aunt looked away. 'I'll make some soup with

plenty of hyssop. We'll have you running about in no time.'

Aarti pulled herself further under the blanket and made her breath heavy.

'You're sure you didn't get up all day?' Aunt quizzed, a frown appearing between her eyebrows.

'No,' Aarti rasped, burying herself into the blankets and letting out a cough.

Aunt stood up and Aarti felt a small coil of tension unravel in her chest. But Aunt didn't move. After a few moments, she turned back round and her expression was hard. 'I don't believe you. I was tidying things in the room next door. The room with private things in it. *My* things. And I forgot the key in the lock. With everything I have to do, I make *one small mistake.*' Her face turned dark red and her eyes flashed with anger. 'You wouldn't be able to resist a poke about in a room with a key hanging from it. DON'T TRY TO TELL ME YOU DIDN'T GO IN!'

Aarti's heart hammered against her chest as Aunt brought her face just centimetres from Aarti's. 'Tell. Me. The. Truth.'

Fierce tears burst from Aarti's eyes and she grasped the rabbit from under her pillow. 'Yes,' she cried. 'I went in and this is what I found. It's mine and you took it away from me.' Aarti knew that things would get bad now but she didn't care. She wanted the shadowy shapes that slumbered in her mind to wake up, and maybe now they would.

Aunt snatched the toy from Aarti's grasp. 'I already told you your parents are dead. Be grateful, Aarti.'

Aarti leapt at Aunt and grabbed the rabbit back, pressed it close. 'It's mine!' She touched the embroidered label and sobbed. 'Why did you lock it away in that room? Who am I and why am I here on this island with nobody but you?' She prepared herself for the punishment. What would it be this time? Sleeping outdoors, night-fishing, or some new thing?

But Aunt's face suddenly clouded over, as if with some difficult emotion. Guilt? 'We have to make the best of things. It's just you and me . . . I only wanted . . .'

'Wanted what?' Aarti knelt on her bed, pleading, tears streaking her face.

'I'll tell you, I will . . . but you're not ready yet,' she murmured, leaving the room. 'I'll call you when the soup's ready.'

Aarti let the salt dry on her face, traced the diamonds on the seahorse brooch and recalled with happiness the day on the beach and how Aunt had tried so hard to make it special. But when she pressed the rabbit to her chest, confused rhythmic sobs drew her into a space deep inside, where the touch of her toy unlocked a memory, the brush of hair soft as silk tickling her skin as she gazed from a cot. The memory tapped like an insistent branch at a window and Aarti looked at the label and willed herself to remember. Where was this place *Nottinghamshire*?

She lay in bed listening as Aunt prepared the soup downstairs. Aarti guessed Aunt didn't really believe she was unwell now, but was just going along with it. Exhausted by all the confusing emotions, Aarti tripped quietly down the stairs when Aunt called her. She sipped the soup silently, watching Aunt for any more clues about how she was feeling, clues to explain the strange look that had passed across her face earlier. But Aunt darted her eyes about the room, wouldn't let them meet Aarti's gaze, and after supper ushered her up to bed.

The next morning Aarti was woken by wind howling down the chimney and rain pelting at the windows. Aarti had spent a restless night, the events of the day before swirling like a tornado through her mind. What would Aunt tell her later, why did she keep her rabbit from her and what was the dread she'd felt so deeply when she'd pressed the toy to her chest? The look on Aunt's face yesterday when Aarti had confronted her . . . it was as if she felt bad about something.

Aunt blustered into Aarti's room and felt her forehead. It was as if nothing had happened. 'Much better,' she said. 'See how my magic soup has done its wonder! Let's take a walk. It will do you good, some fresh air and exercise.'

So everything was back to normal, and even though Aarti wanted to rage against Aunt and force her to tell her the truth, she knew there was nothing she could do to make this happen.

'You wear the waterproof, Aarti,' said Aunt, after breakfast. She draped the coat over Aarti's shoulders. 'And I shall wear my extra-thick jersey.'

'But Aunt,' Aarti began. 'The rain and wind are too fierce . . .'

'What?'

Aarti knew there was no use. 'Nothing.' Her breath tied a knot in her throat.

'Good. So zip up and let's go.'

Fear gripped Aarti as the wind pressed against her body and she struggled along behind Aunt. Rain slanted on to the house. The sky was steel-darkened grey, hanging heavy over the chimneys, pouring against the patched-up holes. There was enough rain in the sky for a whole week, a whole month even. The chickens were quiet inside their coop, water cascading over its rooftop and down the sides like a waterfall.

'We'll head for the cliffs,' yelled Aunt. 'A clifftop walk is what we need. It'll blow away the cobwebs.'

Aarti tucked her plait into the hood and pulled it down close by her head.

'Come on then,' shouted Aunt. 'Keep up.' Already Aunt was drenched, the jumper hanging heavy, her yellow hair plastered to her head.

Aarti tensed her jaw, lifting her eyes to the lightning flashing overhead.

They turned their backs on the house. Rain fell like bullets through the dark clouds and ran like a river on the ground, making muddy tracks that splashed on to Aarti's trailing coat.

Drips fell from the hood on to her nose, trickled down her chin and snaked under her clothes, making shivery goosebumps.

Aunt stormed ahead. 'Bracing weather, this,' she laughed. 'Washes away your sleepy head. Isn't it marvellous?'

'Y . . . yes,' said Aarti, fear of angering Aunt making her stomach fold in on itself. She knew it was best to agree when Aunt was in this mood. The last time she had murmured only a tired sigh in response to Aunt's enthusiasm, Aunt had turned on her and made her run barefoot laps around the frozen winter field. The snow had bitten sores into the soles of her feet until she no longer felt them, and when she came in blood pulsed like a dragon's breath through her toes and the itchy welts burst painfully.

Aarti swallowed at the memory as they wound their way along the edge of the forest, past bare branched trees and gnarled old yews, until they were on the other side of the island.

Aarti was out of breath and her legs were tired by the time the cliffs appeared, dipping precariously below them. Thunder rumbled across the thick slate clouds.

Aunt ran on ahead towards the sea. 'Aarti,' she shouted, the rain slashing on to her. 'Isn't it wonderful? So pure and fresh and beautiful!'

'We should be careful,' said Aarti, keeping back from the slippery edge.

'That's your problem.' Aunt stopped and turned to face her. 'You're too cautious. You should embrace this landscape.' She threw her arms up to the sky and the rain fell even more heavily.

The wild sea spat and leapt against the rocks below the cliff as if it wanted to claw its way to the land.

'Come on,' said Aunt, continuing along the edge.

Aarti followed a few paces behind, the wind whipping the hood from her head, the coat pressed flat against her chest.

'Aunt!' cried Aarti, her voice faint against the wind and muffled by the rain.

'We'll see if we can find any eagle eggs,' said Aunt Amalie. 'I never understand why you never come back with any.'

'But Aunt,' said Aarti. 'It's too dangerous!'

'Nonsense,' replied Aunt, grasping the edge of the grey rock and lowering herself down the cliff. 'I'll show you how it's done.'

Aarti watched as Aunt disappeared below the cliff edge and found a foothold. Sea spray rose from the water below, drenching Aunt with an icy blast, the unrelenting rain battering her from above.

'There's an eyrie just here,' she shouted, moving sideways across the face of the cliff. 'And three eggs!'

Aarti stayed away from the edge but peered over, her heart hammering as fear gripped her chest. 'Aunt, come back!'

Aunt reached into a hole in the rock, stretching. 'See? Nearly there!' she shouted.

'Aunt Amalie!' cried Aarti. She crouched down near the edge, buried her fingers in the wet grass, holding on against the storm. 'Stop!'

Aunt slipped as an enormous gust of wind tugged at her jumper. Aarti watched, powerless, as Aunt tried to clutch at the rock, but the stone was slick with rain and her fingers slid away from the cliff face.

Her eyes met Aarti's, wide with fear. Aarti's heart rammed against her chest.

Aunt let out a shrill scream and her gold hair sprang into the air as she fell down the sheer rock. Aarti covered her eyes, but she already knew the scream, nearly drowned out by the crashing waves on the rocks below, would ring in her ears for ever.

9

Aarti forced herself to her feet and sprinted further along the clifftop until she reached a craggy, windblown tree, blood thundering at her temples. She anchored herself among its roots, gazed down at the rocks, frantically scanning the area where Aunt must have fallen, but all she could see was the white swell of the sea as it beat against the island, pulling everything down into its dark, swirling grasp.

Aarti stared at the giant waves. Rain dripped into her eyes, mingling with the sea salt. The wind continued to batter her body as she leant against the tree, a numb feeling spreading through her.

'Aunt,' she whispered, the word she'd repeated every day on the island, the word that had meant the world to her. She was her adoptive mother, despite everything. She called again into the storm. 'Aunt!'

The name clung to her tongue before parting and rising into the wild storm.

She didn't know what to do or how she felt . . . she'd wished to be free of Aunt so many times, but not like this – she hadn't wished her harm. When Aarti shut her eyes, she remembered that perfect day they'd had, the diamond brooch sparkling on the beach, the jumper – A for Aarti. A for Amalie. A for Aunt. She was the only mother she knew and now she was gone too, just like her first.

A thought drifted like a feather floating slowly into her brain – she really was completely alone now. She thought of the letters she'd found from Aunt to her parents, how lonely and homesick she'd felt. A confused sadness rose inside Aarti as a fat tear rolled down her cheek. She couldn't do this. She was going to be so alone.

She tried to hold her body still but it sprang out of control, shook like brittle leaves in the wind. Staring at the raging sea below, she watched as it hammered with torrential force against the rocks. 'Aunt!' she screamed. 'Aunt!'

But there was no reply.

What was she going to do now? How would she know what to do all by herself?

The thought knocked into her and spread like

fire, catching bit by bit at the corners of her mind until hopelessness overwhelmed her. Her legs buckled. She slipped to the sodden ground, curled into a frozen ball, and burrowed her cheek into the musky earth. She wished she could sink down into it and live in its safety.

When Aarti got so cold that she couldn't feel the tips of her fingers or toes, she forced herself to stand up and dragged herself home.

By the time the house appeared before her, the rain had begun to ease and the wind had dropped – it was hard to tell the time exactly, as the sun was hidden behind a blank veil of grey cloud. Chand was sitting under the walnut tree, the bright moon-mark shining on his forehead. He trotted to her side, rubbed his red tail against her wet coat. She felt like a frozen block of ice and her fingers would barely bend to turn the latch on the door. She leant her shoulder against the jamb and Chand slipped inside ahead of her, mewling and lifting his deep eyes to hers. He'd never come in before. It was as if he knew Aunt was gone.

She dropped her dripping coat and collapsed on the stone floor of the hall, shock pinning her down, fear still racing, filling her limbs with heaviness.

When Aarti woke, the sun arced low through the windows – it was late afternoon. The fire had slumped and white ash had made a powdery bed where logs had been laid earlier by Aunt, before . . .

The shrill scream rang through her mind again. She flinched.

But she had to get up. She had to build the fire again – it was all up to her now. There was still a glimmering glow in the hearth and she cupped her hands together and blew it awake, Chand watching her intently. She piled logs den-like around the embers and blew until the flame flickered red and licked at the dry bark.

'I can do this,' Aarti told Chand. 'See?'

Chand yipped in agreement.

She sat down in front of the flames for a few moments, Chand at her side. As soon as she was still, sadness flooded her – and yet, for the first time since she could ever remember, she didn't feel the tug of nerves, or listen for the sound of heavy footsteps around the house, or worry that she'd done something wrong. She had to admit, although she was sad and scared, she felt something else too.

Relief.

Next, Aarti checked the range and heaved some

fresh logs on. They crackled and blazed. Of course she could do this. She filled the kettle with water and put it on to boil. A hollow emptiness in her stomach made a growl – she hadn't eaten all day! – and, feeling reckless, she dropped all five eggs from the storeroom into a pan.

She assembled a tray of mint tea, a hunk of oat bread and the eggs, and crammed in the food in big mouthfuls while Chand curled by her feet.

She watched the orange flames leap in the hearth as the sun sank outside, the smoky scent rising up the chimney like incense.

Everything was up to Aarti now. She would choose what to do and when to do it. Aunt had taught her well and she knew she could do everything she needed to keep herself fed and warm. She wouldn't kill the chickens or sheep as Aunt had tried to make her – she could live just as well on vegetables from the garden and the eggs and milk they gave; she didn't need to eat meat.

'And with you here,' she said to Chand, 'I'm not even really alone, am I?'

Chand gave a little yelp and settled more comfortably against Aarti's feet.

But with Aunt gone, how would she get the answers she so terribly needed? Had Aunt taken the truth about Aarti's past to her grave?

Aarti tugged at her jumper in agitation before it slowly dawned on her that she could go anywhere in the house now, search the locked room to see what was hidden there, explore Aunt's bedroom that she'd only ever seen from the doorway, and maybe uncover whatever secrets Aunt had been keeping.

She left the glowing hall and quietly walked upstairs, Chand following close behind. When she got to Aunt's room she stepped inside, the familiar smell startling her.

It felt as if Aunt would be back any minute. Jumpers were neatly stacked on the chair, trousers and tunics draped across the back. The bed was made and a thick velvet quilt thrown on top, its ruby red colour matching the thick rug on the floor.

The bedside table was piled with books, titles like *How to Survive in the Wilderness, Islands and Mountains of Scotland, Edible Herbs and Berries, Sailing.* There was a photograph in a small silver frame of a girl about Aarti's age with freckles and a halo of yellow ringlets. On her left was a man with sweptback hair the same colour as the girl's, and on her right a woman with curly dark hair and pale eyes. They were all smiling. Was this Aunt and her parents, the ones who had sent her away to school and made her so unhappy? Aarti put the photo down and picked up the other one, a black-and-white dog bouncing up. Was this Seasalt, who she'd asked after in the letters?

Aarti glanced down at Chand. Aunt might've had a cruel streak, but she was a girl once too – a girl with a friend like Chand. A girl who, though she'd had parents, had believed herself so very alone.

It was late and Aarti suddenly felt enormously tired. She dragged her feet to her own room and threw herself under the blanket. She would search the room tomorrow.

She held her toy rabbit and gently touched Aunt's brooch pinned to his chest. She couldn't stop the tears. 'Aunt,' she breathed. She remembered how things had been when she was small: happy trips to the beach, painting together, how Aunt shared her love for the island . . . She let her eyes close.

Chand spread himself across her feet and together they slept until morning.

Aarti woke with a start, thinking she heard Aunt calling her and that she was late for something. But when she opened her eyes, she remembered what had happened.

Chand stirred at the foot of the bed and yawned. Together they walked down the stairs, Aarti lifting the latch on the front door and letting him out. He turned his head as if to say he'd be back, and trotted off to do the fox things he needed to.

After a breakfast of leftover soup, Aarti did the chores as usual. She opened the coop door and let the chickens out, pushed her hand into the laying box and collected five more eggs, grasped the heavy axe between her slender fingers and with all her might chopped more wood – normally Aunt's job. The effort exhausted her but she knew that this was more important than ever now.

Back inside, Aarti rushed upstairs and searched Aunt's room for the key to the locked room. As she searched, she kept glancing over her shoulder at the door – it felt as if Aunt would appear any minute to punish her for breaking the rules. But of course, she never did. Eventually, Aarti found the key hidden in a mother-of-pearl box on the dressing table.

She hurried out, hands trembling, slotted the key in the lock and entered the secret room again. Sunbeams danced on the boxes, as if inviting Aarti to explore. She looked through the clutter slowly and methodically, searching for clues to what had happened in the past.

She found a box of maps, a framed photo of Aunt as a child in ballet clothes, dancing in front of a crowd, and a yellowing certificate stating 'First Class Degree Economics' with Aunt's name in curling script across the top. She found more dusty photos in brown envelopes – including a picture of Aunt as a young woman collecting something from a stage, shaking hands and smiling, all dressed up in a glitzy outfit. She found, too, a photo of Aunt's parents older and frailer in front of the house, and a few letters inside a cardboard folder.

Aarti held one of the letters and read:

Amalie dear, both Pa and I are sorry to hear that you have not been feeling well lately. It is such a shame after you were doing so well. Your job in the london bank sounds good. You have made enough money now I expect with all the awards you have been getting. I know things have been hard for you but you must try to control your temper, Amalie — you never were a people person.

Come back to the island, we could do with your help . . .

'You must try to control your temper . . .' Aarti murmured out loud. *I guess Aunt always had problems with her temper*, she thought sadly. But she wasn't here to find out about Aunt. She was here to find her own secrets. What was it that Aunt had said she would tell her, one day? There must be some clues here.

Aarti frantically rummaged through more boxes — there had to be something to explain the memories that had been rising up inside her . . . the garden, the smells, the woman who held her. There must be more in here, something more than a toy rabbit, to give her the answers she needed.

But all she found were documents, mainly, and more photos, and old clothes which she guessed might've belonged to Aunt's parents. Finally, in an official-looking wallet she found a thick piece of paper embossed with a red stamp – this seemed important. It was typed and said that in case something happened to Amalie Macdonald the island should be passed to her niece Aarti Macdonald. She smiled. Aunt had always told her the island would be hers – whatever she was hiding, she hadn't lied about that. She put the wallet beside the open door and carried on searching.

But even though Aarti searched until the day began to fade, she didn't find answers to any of her questions. There had been nothing in the room about her past, after all. Nothing but Squidgy Rabbit. Aunt had told the truth: it really was her own private stuff. She collected the wallet and left the room, bitterly disappointed. What was she supposed to do next? There wasn't anything else to discover in this house.

Later, Chand scratched at the door and Aarti let him in. 'Would you like some pumpkin seeds?' She stroked the moon shape between his eyes and he trotted close behind as she went to the store.

Above the door, Aarti noticed a small dark patch. She frowned, pushed it open and gasped. A long wet trail started at the top of the ceiling and had trickled down into the rough-spun bags of oats and flour

Aunt had stored on the shelves.

She checked each bag carefully, her hands shaking as they sank into the soggy mulch. Why hadn't she checked before? But even if she had, she realized, it probably would've been too late. 'Another leak in the roof,' she whispered, her voice thick with horror. 'Chand . . . it's all ruined.' She felt the envelopes with seeds for planting; they too were damp and had begun to turn mouldy.

The storm which had whipped Aunt from the cliffs had obviously damaged the abbey too.

Chand rubbed his head sympathetically against her leg as Aarti sank down to the storeroom floor, her mind spinning. *Don't panic*, she thought over and over, *don't panic*. She still had fresh food – eggs, sheep's milk, vegetables and herbs from the garden and whatever else she could forage on the island. Then there were the preserves from last winter, tightly sealed in glass jars, protected from water – plus a decent amount of oats and flour, and even some pumpkin seeds, set aside in the kitchen cupboards. She would be all right for a while now that spring was here. Soon, the food she'd find outside would be enough to live on.

But I'll never survive next winter, she realized, a cold sinking feeling knotting in her tummy.

She forced herself up, brought a bucket to catch the drips in the store and afterwards made eggs and fritters and ate them by the fire. They snoozed a while and Aarti wondered if she should do her ballet practice even though there was no need now. But she didn't feel like it – worries about the ruined supplies circled round and round her mind. And the roof . . . Aunt had never taught her how to fix it. She'd have to get rid of the ruined supplies and bring what was left into the kitchen.

To distract herself, she opened up the map she'd brought from the room upstairs and spread it before the fire. In the corner it said 'The British Isles'.

She scoured the drawing to see if she could find Nottinghamshire. The map had sections dividing it up and she traced her finger from the top to the bottom searching for the place where her cuddly rabbit had come from – where *she* had come from. And then she found it, bordered by Derbyshire and Leicestershire. Next she found Scotland – Aunt had always said they lived in the Scottish wilds – and then she studied the islands off the Scottish coast. There were lots of them, some just tiny dots. Which one was she on? She folded the map; it didn't seem that having it was going to help with anything. But it had made her realize something: if she wasn't going to find answers on the island, she would have to leave it.

The thought clanged in her head loud as a church bell, and she felt as if a sudden wave had crashed into her, waking her up. Her heart tangled with fear and sadness. But Aarti knew it was up to her now – she *had* to find a way off the island, a way to uncover the secrets of her past. And she had to do so before winter. Because if she didn't, without the food in the storeroom, she'd starve.

Chand pushed his muzzle against Aarti's arm and let out an insistent mewling. He ran from the hall to the front door and back again.

'What is it, Chand? Do you want to go out again?' She opened the door into the calm, clear dusk but still he sat staring back at her. 'So you want us to go for a walk, is that it?' She grabbed her coat and followed him out, slipping a box of matches and a candle into her pocket. Somehow she knew where Chand would lead her.

The evening had turned into night by the time they arrived at the waterfall, the moon shining bright into the water. Inside the shrine, she lit her candle, opened her Krishna book at her favourite page and looked at his beautiful smile. It was as if he could actually see her and it made her feel less alone. Maybe she could make another wish. She read his poem aloud, felt she understood it more – in her own way.

'. . . *I am the pure fragrance in earth and brightness of fire.*'

She guessed it was telling her there was the power of nature on the island and this blue god Krishna *was* the island. If he was all around her, maybe he would listen to her, maybe he could help her. She'd asked for the truth once before and she'd found Squidgy Rabbit – maybe she could get even closer to the truth this time, if she wished hard enough.

Aarti put her palms together, closed her eyes and asked for help to survive.

Summer

11

Time passed and slowly Aarti got used to being alone. She brought her Krishna book back from the shrine and set it up to one side of the table, lighting beeswax candles around it. Reading it comforted her and seemed to give her days a purpose that wasn't only about surviving.

She'd need to leave before her supplies ran out, to search for her answers over the sea, but it wasn't that simple – she didn't know how she could do it. Aunt had never mentioned a boat and even if there was one, Aarti had no idea how to sail. Besides, surviving the last gasp of the harsh spring took every minute of her time – at the end of each day she'd drop into her bed, exhausted, Chand curled at her feet.

One day when the long shadows of spring had faded and the island was spinning back to life, when the sun was beginning to warm the blue sea and turn the leaves bright, Chand didn't come home. Aarti wasn't worried. She left the door ajar and let the early summer scents into the house – but Chand never showed up. The next day, she walked for a while around the island, intermittently calling his name. He didn't come and he wasn't waiting by the walnut tree. Maybe he was busy with his fox family.

But by the third night she knew something was wrong; he had never left her for so long. A knot of worry uncurled itself and leapt into her throat where it turned into a howl as she rushed out of the house, calling his name between sobs.

'Chand! Chand!' she shouted, as she ran to the walnut tree, its blurry outline rippling with leaves. The ground at the foot of the trunk remained empty. Her chest tightened. What if he was hurt and he couldn't find his way home?

She hurried into the woods, the owls hooting in the dusky evening, searching all the usual tracks and trails they liked to explore. She hunted until her legs ached and her breath beat ragged from her lungs, but she didn't find him anywhere. Not even in the cave behind the waterfall.

Here, bitter tears tracked down her salty cheeks and an emptiness stretched itself through her body. 'How could this have happened?' she cried at her shrine. 'I ask for help but instead the thing I love most is taken away.'

She dragged herself back towards the harbour and the beach, the full moon spreading its silver rays over the sea, the stars twinkling between the clouds. She climbed up to the four standing stones on the hill and breathed in the cold night air. She let herself slip on to the damp ground and leant against the hard stone, allowed her eyelids to shut. 'What happened to him?' she murmured, as a wave of tiredness swept over her and pulled her into sleep.

She woke in the middle of the night, a shiver sweeping through her body, confusion spreading like a groggy dream, and she struggled to understand why she had woken up outside. And then the hammer of her missing friend thudded hard against her ribs and she felt his loss all over again.

She swiped another tear from her face and turned to leave for home, but the silver shadow of the moon caught her eye and she thought she saw something flash quick as lightning down on the beach. 'Chand?' she called tenderly.

A strange flutter snapped in her stomach as she stepped down from the safety of the giant stones and walked across the wet sand towards the edge of the dark, frothing sea.

She stared out across the water and saw something under the rippling tide. Maybe she was imagining things, but when she looked again more closely, she knew she wasn't mistaken.

There was something floating on the peppermint dark sea, caught in the light of the moon. Was it a fish – or maybe a seal?

No . . . it was definitely a person, floating on their back.

Aarti waded out, panic gripping her lungs. In the moonlight the figure's blue skin appeared to be patterned with swirling shapes, like ink tattoos spiralled across its face.

Grey-winged fulmars rose up from the water in a sudden flapping, raucous cloud as she dipped her arms into the cold sea around the figure. Heart thrumming, she caught hold of its shoulders and pulled the body towards the beach. As she started to clear the water, the body became a leaden weight and she lost her grip, toppling back and landing in the shallows. The birds cackled and followed her, swooping and diving as she stooped again. She dragged the person on to the sand against the push and pull of the tide, pausing to catch her breath and rest, and kept pulling until she finally collapsed beside it, her breath hoarse.

The moon caught the silver flute which was strung around the figure's neck. The blue tattoo-like markings had disappeared from the pale skin – a trick of the sea, she thought. Aarti leant over the figure anxiously – no, not the *figure*: the *boy*! Her breath quickened.

Aunt had filled her mind with all the bad things that boys could do. They were bullies and worse, she'd said, and they always let you down . . . but Aarti had never met a boy. She'd read stories about boys though, and they weren't all bad – just like the girls weren't all good – and besides, this boy needed her help.

She pressed her ear lightly against his chest and heard a faint beating heart – and a gurgling sound in his throat. Instinctively, she turned him to his side and sea water spluttered from his mouth and nose, and he took a deep gravelly breath.

She jumped away, startled. 'Who are you?' she whispered.

He didn't speak, only opened his dark eyes. Clouds covered the moon and his face darkened too, once more tinged a startling blue-green with tattoo-like patterns, black hair plastered against his face. But in a blink, the cloud passed and his face was clear once again. He appeared to be struggling to focus on her face. She swallowed and knew if she wanted him to survive she had to get him home.

She threaded her arm under his and made him sit up. The cold wind was beginning to blow and she shivered.

Aarti struggled to lift him to his feet until he was standing unsteadily, his head a touch higher than hers. She looped her arm around his back and slowly shuffled him towards home. He kept closing his eyes, wavering. Soon Aarti was warm with the effort of keeping him upright.

Aarti thought talking to him might help keep him awake. 'Y-you're safe now,' she stuttered. 'I'm going to get you warm.' He kept closing his eyes, leaning into her. 'There's a big fire burning at home and soup. Come on, just a little further.'

He didn't respond, but scraping one foot in front of the other, they eventually arrived back at the abbey, Aarti's head swimming with questions.

Even though her nerves jangled, part of her was excited to have someone with her at last. With Aunt dead and Chand lost, she'd started to think she might live here alone for ever – but now . . . She opened the front door and eased the boy inside.

Exhausted, Aarti took him into the hall and settled him by the fire. With shaky hands, she stripped off most of his soaking clothes and placed the silver flute on the table. She dragged the red velvet quilt from Aunt's room and bundled him up in it.

Aarti fetched the soup that she always kept warming in the oven and began feeding the boy small spoonfuls, but he drowsily pushed her hand away.

'No,' she said firmly. 'You have to eat. This is good, it will help you.' She rested the spoon on his lip and slowly he opened his mouth and let the soup trickle in.

He kept his eyes closed but at last his face began to lose its ghostly look, the fire lighting it up and making it seem golden.

Aarti fetched comfrey balm and with a gentle touch dabbed it on his face and hands, on his wrists and neck, wherever she could see cuts and grazes.

Aarti's questions crammed into her mouth, but she knew she should wait until morning. It made her happy that he had eaten the soup and that she was helping him to get well. She went upstairs and brought down some of her clothes: a thick jumper, trousers and socks. She decided she would stay in the hall so she could keep an eye on him and brought her blanket down.

She stared hard at his sleeping face. She couldn't

believe there was another human being right next to her. Despite Aunt's words about the cruelty of men ringing through her head, she thought he looked kind.

Aarti woke to the sound of birds outside. She kept her eyes closed for a moment longer, savouring her dream of being with Chand. When at last she opened them, she peeped over her blanket at the boy, who was still sleeping. Her eyes shifted to the silver flute that lay on the table and she thought what a strange thing it was to carry tied around your neck.

She examined him carefully, tucking her face under the edge of the blanket. Last night in the shadows of the moon it had been hard to get a proper look. He seemed about her age, his black wavy hair skimming his shoulders, freckles peppering his pale skin.

Trying not to wake him, she placed more wood on the fire and the range, took some oatmeal from the big glass jar on the countertop and made two bowls of porridge. She topped each with preserved pears from last autumn's harvest and sprinkled them with pumpkin seeds.

The boy started, flashed open his eyes in alarm and stared at Aarti.

'It's OK,' she said, more confidently than she felt. 'Don't be scared . . . you were washed up on the beach. I found you, rescued you, last night.'

The boy continued to stare. His eyes were as brown as a smooth-backed hare, and he seemed not to see Aarti, but looked beyond her at something else.

'Your clothes are still a bit damp,' she said. 'But you can wear these.' She patted the clothes she'd brought down yesterday, neatly folded in a pile beside him. 'And I made porridge. I expect you're hungry.'

The boy still didn't speak, but his eyes started to droop. Even so, she felt her stomach give a twist. Not the kind that happened around Aunt but a new feeling of excitement, of having someone to talk to at last, someone special, maybe a friend.

12

The boy lay with his eyes closed, in the thick bundle of red velvet quilt by the fire. Over the next four days, Aarti woke him and fed him soup and mashed egg with plenty of herb teas, but he never spoke, his eyes droopy as if he was half asleep – and the rest of the time he slept. On the fifth day he woke properly at last.

He was dazed and looked around slowly, scanning the room and peering at Aarti as she busied herself fetching the morning porridge and a drink of steaming nettle tea.

She placed them on the table. 'You're awake at last. I . . . I'll take my blanket up,' she said. 'And you can get changed and then we can have breakfast – and if you feel up to it – you can tell me who you are and what happened.' Aarti knew she was talking really fast, but she'd been waiting and waiting for

94

him to wake up.

He gave a small smile that filled Aarti with relief.

She rolled her blanket and took it upstairs. In her bedroom she picked up her Squidgy Rabbit and pressed him to her chest. 'Remember the boy I told you about, Squidgy? Well, he's woken up! I can't believe that there's an actual person downstairs.' She felt the label with the address on it again. 'He might know more about this place.' She felt excitement and hope lighting a flame inside her, and for the first time in ages she felt truly happy. She tucked Squidgy into the bed with the blanket under his chin and planted a kiss on his forehead.

When she got downstairs the boy was dressed in her clothes, the blue knitted jumper and loose grey trousers. His slim wrists poked out from the ends of the sleeves and the trousers flapped about his calves.

He was standing by the fire, staring into the flames, and when he saw Aarti in the doorway he looked up. 'Thank you for the porridge.'

She blinked, surprised to hear his voice for the first time. One of the porridge bowls on the table was empty. 'You're welcome. You can change into your own clothes whenever you like,' she said. 'They're dry. Drink your tea, nettles give you strength.' She walked across to the table, sat down and began eating her own porridge.

The boy sat opposite, cupped his fingers round the mug and sipped the hot, earthy drink.

'My name's Aarti, what's yours?'

'It's Euan, Euan Macleod.'

'You were lucky I found you, Euan Macleod,' Aarti said. 'What happened?'

He frowned. 'I can't really remember much. Everything is a blur.'

Aarti was worried by how his face paled at the question. 'That's OK. Don't think too much just now. Maybe you'll remember more later and then you can tell me, but only if you want to, if you feel like it.'

'OK.' He smiled at her gratefully.

Aarti's gaze slid down to the flute he wore around his neck. 'I'd love to hear you play?' she suggested gently.

Euan took the silver flute and put it on the table. He stared at it as if he didn't recognize it at all and his eyes took on a distant look, as if he was thinking of another place far from here.

Aarti quickly changed the subject; Euan might be feeling physically better but he was obviously dealing with a lot. 'When you start to feel up to it, I'll show you the island. It's beautiful, and now that summer's here it changes and comes alive.'

A frown appeared on Euan's forehead as he looked through the doorway. 'Where's your family?'

Aarti swallowed and tapped her spoon against her bowl. 'I lived here with my aunt until a few months ago, but . . . she died.'

The boy's eyebrows lifted in surprise. 'So . . . you're living all alone? Is that allowed?'

'Allowed?' Aarti shook her head, not understanding. 'That's just the way it is. There isn't anyone else living on the island.'

Euan was silent for a moment, as if he was struggling to process Aarti's words. 'I'm sorry about your aunt,' he said eventually. 'How did she die?'

'It was during a storm. She slipped off a cliff into the sea,' Aarti said, keeping her voice matter-of-fact.

'Do you . . . miss her?' Euan asked gently.

Aarti nodded. 'In a way. She loved me and cared for me all my life. And she was the only person I knew. In another way . . . I feel a little relieved. She could be . . . I mean, sometimes she was quite unkind.' Being able to say this out loud at last brought all the years of pain flooding back.

'OK,' Euan said, frowning.

Aarti continued quickly. 'Actually, I had a friend until a week ago – he was called Chand. He was a fox. But one night he didn't come home.' Tears bubbled from Aarti's eyes and she wiped them away. 'I'm glad you're here, Euan. Being truly alone before you arrived . . . that was hard.'

'Don't cry.' Euan touched her arm but the kindness of the gesture made her cry even harder. 'Do you want to talk?'

And Aarti found that she did. She told him everything. How she'd lived on the island as long as she could remember; how she'd started to recall things she thought might be from a time before; how Aunt had gotten worse recently; how hard life had become. She spilt out all the things Aunt forced her to do and all the punishments that waited for her if she managed to anger her.

She told him about the good things too: how Aunt had taken her to the beach on her special day and gifted her the precious brooch, how she was capable of tenderness and love and how that made her cruelty even harder to bear. She told him about the leak too, how all the stored oats and flour had been ruined. And all the time Euan listened carefully, his gentle eyes still and full of thought.

Finally she wiped her sore cheeks and stood up. 'I want to show you something. I'll bring it down.'

Aarti fetched Squidgy Rabbit from her bedroom

and shyly held him out to Euan. 'This is mine, but my aunt kept it from me. My parents died when I was little and Aunt adopted me, but I don't understand why she would hide this if that was the full story – why she wouldn't even tell me who they were.'

Euan reached across and took Squidgy Rabbit.

'He's a bit dirty, he was locked in a room for years, but there's this label, look.'

Euan peered down at the message under Squidgy Rabbit's arm.

My name is Squidgy Rabbit –
if I'm lost please return to Lantern Hall,
Blackberry Lane, Nottinghamshire

'Do you know where that is?' asked Aarti, stepping closer to Euan. 'I found Nottinghamshire on the map but I thought you might know more.'

'N . . . no. I mean, I've heard of Nottinghamshire too. But I don't know about the rest of the address. Sorry.'

Aarti took her toy back, her heart sinking. 'That's OK.'

Euan scratched his eyebrow like he didn't know what to say. His face clouded over and a deep furrow appeared between his eyes that suddenly sparked with worry. 'My family . . . how will I tell my family that I'm alive? They'll be worried sick. Do you have a phone?'

Aarti didn't know what to say. She shook her head. 'We're completely cut off here, I'm so sorry.' The evening turned dark as both of them stared into the fire like an answer was hiding in the orange flames and Euan's face appeared somehow different, blue shadows casting a strange glow over him.

Aarti moved over to the open book about Indian mythology and, taking a splint of wood, poked it in the fire and lit the candle like she had on every night while the boy slept.

'What's that?' he asked, peering at the page that was propped open.

'It's one of my favourite books.' She glanced over to the shelves that were overflowing with books. 'There are hundreds of them here, books about everything. It's how I feel connected to the world beyond the island.'

Euan frowned. 'Stories are made up though . . . you know that? They don't show you what the real world is like. Besides, all of these books look old.'

Aarti felt her face redden. 'Maybe that's a good thing. Aunt said the real world is cruel and that people hurt you, that I was better off here away from it all, that she protected me from it.' Aarti felt a painful knot in her throat, her voice sharp. 'Besides, not all of these books are stories. Lots of them are about true things.'

'Sorry,' Euan said. 'I didn't mean to upset you.'

Aarti pushed down the feelings in her chest. 'No, I'm sorry. It's just . . . these books mean a lot to me. But will you tell me what it's like, in the world across the seas?'

'Sure.' Euan came to stand beside her and flicked through the pages of the book of the blue gods. The painting of Krishna reflected its rich blue tones on to Euan's face, and for a moment he looked like he was trying to catch hold of a memory that he was drawing towards himself like a flickering moth to light.

He concentrated on reading the poem in the book, the strange one Aarti had memorized, all about how nature was part of the god Krishna, the flowing rivers, the mountains and the seas.

'My ma's really into the ancient gods of Scotland. She's got books and books about the Druids. There's a poem she framed and put on the wall in our kitchen . . . it's just like this one.' He began to recite it:

'*I am the Wind that blows across the Sea*
I am the Wave of the Ocean

I am the Murmur of the Billows
I am the Bull of the Seven Combats
I am the Vulture on the Rock
I am a Ray of the Sun
I am the Fairest of the Flowers . . .'

To Aarti's surprise, a tear smudged down Euan's cheek and he sat down at the table. 'She used to read it to me, it's from thousands of years ago. It tells of the very first time this Druid, Amergin, stepped from the sea on to the land.'

Aarti drew closer to him. 'You must miss her a lot. I'm really sorry you're stuck here.'

Euan sniffed, nodded slightly and began coughing. He clearly wasn't fully recovered; Aarti would have to keep an eye on him.

'Here,' Aarti said gently, 'reading this always makes me feel better.'

She began reciting the lines she knew by heart from the Krishna poem, and the yellow candle flame seemed to flicker in time to the words as calm spread slowly through Aarti. The two of them sat surrounded by the glow that seemed to wrap itself around them, binding them in a circle of friendship.

13

'We have to find a way to get off the island,' said Euan the next morning as he shovelled porridge into his mouth. 'I need to get home.'

'I wish it was that easy,' Aarti said. 'I want to leave too; I don't think I'll find any answers about my past here – I've looked everywhere. Plus, there's no way we'd survive winter without the ruined food from the leak. But . . .' She took a deep, shuddering breath. 'But Euan, there's no way to leave. We're stuck.'

Euan raised an eyebrow. 'That's not possible. Your aunt must have got here somehow. There must be a boat.'

Aarti felt her cheeks heat up. 'If there was a boat, I would have found it by now, don't you think? I've been all over the island. And Aunt never mentioned one.'

'But she wouldn't, necessarily, would she? If she

didn't want to leave, I mean,' Euan suggested. 'And there must be some hiding places you don't know about. Didn't you tell me there was a cave Aunt had never found? Well, what if she had a secret hiding place too?'

Aarti felt a prickle of uneasiness. Aunt *had* hidden Squidgy Rabbit from her – what else could she have kept from Aarti? Could it be something as big as a boat?

She bit the skin at the corner of her thumb. 'You still haven't told me what happened,' she said, after a pause. 'I mean, how you got here. Don't *you* have a boat?'

'It all feels so mixed up and strange,' he began. 'There's lots that I can't remember, and what's left is a blur . . . but I know I wanted to go fishing with my da. He was busy so I didn't tell him and went alone. I have a wee boat, she's called *Dunter*, named for the porpoises that swim about the waters. She's small but fast and safe . . . except this day a huge storm blew up. It wasn't expected. All I remember is the waves getting higher and higher and being pushed further out to sea, away from land, then nothing until I was washed up here when you rescued me.'

Aarti frowned. 'So why did you have a flute with you?'

He glanced down at the instrument around his neck. 'I know this is going to sound strange but I've no idea.' He laughed. 'I can't even play the flute.'

Aarti didn't know what to say. Perhaps the storm and sea had messed with his memory.

Euan's face grew serious again. 'They'll be so worried, my ma and da, they'll think I've drowned out at sea.' He turned to face Aarti. 'We have to get away from here, please. Let's just look for a boat – what harm can it do?' He began coughing.

'You're still not well.'

'It's just a little cough – come on, let's see what we can find.'

'OK, I'll show you around,' Aarti said.

After they'd finished eating, Aarti fetched warm clothes from upstairs and they quickly wrapped up and left the house.

'You've got sheep,' said Euan, looking over at the field behind the house, his face clouding again. 'We have a farm too.'

'They give us so much. Milk, wool for knitting and weaving into cloth, meat too, but I can never bear to eat it. I used to hide it in my pocket so Aunt wouldn't see.'

'My da says it's a way of life. Things get eaten . . .

but I know what you mean, when the wee lambs come out all fluffy and cute, hard to not keep seeing their faces staring at you from the plate.'

The sun rose golden over the abbey rooftop, a blue sky mottled white with fluffy clouds spread ahead of them. Blackbirds swooped in and out of the budding branches, collecting strands of grass and tufts of wool to line their nests, the tapping sound of woodpeckers egging them on.

'Let's try down by the beach first,' Euan said.

Aarti thought she knew the island so well, but were there really places she didn't know about, a place where Aunt could have hidden a boat? She remembered times when they went walking and the mists came down, and somehow everything turned mysterious and different and they would arrive by some magic in a place that Aarti didn't recognize. And there were some places on the island that Aunt had said she shouldn't wander in, on the furthest edges, where the sea came pouncing like a hungry tiger.

The salty breeze greeted them as the ruffled waves came into view, the blue sea stretching out towards the line of the horizon, broad-winged fulmars gliding centimetres above the waves.

'Is this where you found me?'

Aarti remembered that Euan hadn't been back before now and he must be feeling the shock again of lying there in the cold water, half alive.

'You were a little way out. I thought at first you were a seal . . . I couldn't see properly and the moon was casting strange shadows.' She remembered the blue pattern on Euan's skin, like a tattoo, but decided not to mention it.

Together they clambered down to the beach, shielded by the rise of the hill behind it and the bulk of the standing stones.

The sand was still damp from the sea that was rushing out on the tide. Euan breathed in a long, deep breath and stared out across the waves. He put his hand to his brow, narrowed his eyes against the sun as if he was searching for his boat, the *Dunter*, or for a glimpse of his land beyond.

'Could there be a place near here where your aunt left a boat?'

'There are caves around the corner, we should search those.' Aarti had explored the caves many times – she already knew they were empty. But she liked how the sense of purpose and fresh air had added colour to Euan's cheeks. There was no harm in humouring him.

They tramped along the sand until they were at

the very far end of the beach. As they reached the caves, Aarti flicked her gaze back at their footprints, zigzagging behind them, and at the tide as it swept them clean to the sea.

14

Puffins hugged tight to the stone, their black-and-white bodies squashed together, sticking out their tubby chests against the gusts of wind.

'Hello, puffins,' said Euan, passing close by. 'No scratching now.'

'And definitely no pecking,' laughed Aarti.

The puffins eyed them for a moment before ignoring them completely and carrying on with their watch of the sea.

Tufts of fresh green sea samphire grew in the cracks further up and Aarti took her small knife and cut a little, storing it in her pocket as she climbed away from the water. 'We can have some with our supper,' she called to Euan, who grabbed at the slippery rocks below her, hauling himself up to stand tall.

'Look, over there,' said Aarti. 'Another cove and caves at the back.'

They leapt down from the rocks on to the soft white sand and ran towards the blank mouths of the caves that bordered the beach.

When they peered inside, they could see pools of dark water, sitting still in hollows of sand.

'This would be a good place to store a boat,' said Euan. 'Easy to get it out and back to sea.' He scanned the darkness eagerly.

'Yes, but this is too simple. I've been down here loads of times – if Aunt wanted to keep the boat secret she'll have put it somewhere else. There's nothing here, Euan.'

'It might just be really well hidden,' he said hopefully.

But after they'd searched the three other caves, Aarti knew Euan had to concede defeat. There was nothing here that could take them away from the island.

A grey cloud on the horizon puffed up and grew larger, moving towards land.

Aarti shivered. 'There's a storm coming, let's head back. I don't think you should get caught in a rain shower, you're only just beginning to feel better.'

But Euan stood with his hands on his hips, the wind blowing his black hair, staring into the cave. 'We'll find the boat, Aarti. Maybe not today but tomorrow or the day after. I'll find my family – and you'll find your answers.'

She kicked hard at the sand. 'If there *is* a boat . . .'

'There is. There has to be. Have faith, Aarti.' Euan put an arm round Aarti's shoulder and she relaxed a little. It was so strange to feel his touch, like he was a brother, someone who cared. It felt so good.

'Let's get back then,' she smiled, 'before the tide cuts us off.'

They retraced their steps over the puffin rocks and back to the harbour, the first drops of early summer rain shaking down from the sky.

By the time they returned to the house, the rain was falling faster and they ducked into the abbey, the smoky fire welcoming them back. Aarti made tea and they warmed themselves by the flames.

'If only the fire could show us where Aunt hid the boat,' said Aarti, watching the orange tongues flick and dart from the hearth, as if they were trying to tell her something.

Euan nodded, then said, 'Do you think there's a map of the island somewhere? We might find some clues about where to look.'

'I drew a map on my bedroom wall, but that's only the places I already know about.' Aarti straightened up – hadn't there been something like that in the locked room? 'Wait here – I think I saw some maps upstairs.'

She returned after a few minutes with the shoebox of maps. 'There might be one in here,' she said.

They sat at the table and emptied the box's contents in front of them. There were four folded maps. Three of them were published maps – one of England, another of Scotland, the third of Wales – but the fourth and final one was different.

Aarti pushed the others to one side and took hold of it. 'This one is really old,' she said, 'and it looks like it's been drawn by hand.' She unfolded it fully, taking care not to rip the thin, aged paper, and laid it on the table.

'It's the island!' she said excitedly, as her eyes roved over the image.

'There's the house,' said Euan, peering closer at the slightly faded ink drawings.

'And the woods at the back of the house,' said Aarti, 'the harbour and the bay.'

'The caves where we went today,' continued Euan. 'It's all been marked on carefully.'

Aarti pointed to the land beyond the cliffs, where the rocks were huge jagged monsters and where the sea came lashing in blue curling ink. 'I think this must be the part of the island where Aunt said I shouldn't try to climb down to the shore, that it was too dangerous.' She pointed to a spot near where a windblown tree had been picked out in sepia. She remembered how she'd clung to it in the moments after Aunt's death. She swallowed, her voice shaking slightly as she continued. 'That's where Aunt told me to collect eggs from . . . and where she fell during the storm. The cliff is sheer and she had no chance once she lost her grip.'

Euan squinted at the faded lines. 'There could be caves down there,' he said quietly. 'I know it's dangerous, Aarti, but I can't see anywhere else on the map that looks like a likely hiding place. There *has* to be a boat there.'

Aarti glanced up, met his eyes and nodded. 'I think we should go and look.'

Rain splatted the windows and thunder rumbled across the roof. But inside, Aarti's heart started to shine with something like hope.

15

When they'd tidied up the map, Aarti and Euan busied themselves with dinner.

'Will you tell me about *your* family?' Aarti asked, a little shyly, as she started to break eggs into the pan. The rain beat harder on the roof. 'I don't really know what it's like to have a mum and dad . . . or brothers or sisters. Do you have siblings?'

Euan started to chop the mushrooms Aarti had brought in from the storeroom. 'I have a ma and pa and a wee sister. We have a farm on the coast. A sheep farm.'

'What's it like having a sister?'

'She can be a little pest at times,' laughed Euan. 'Her name is Mhairi and she's six. She always wants to come with me, tags along when I go rounding up the sheep with our dog Saaban, then she gets tired and I have to give her a piggyback.' He rolled his eyes affectionately and Aarti laughed. The mushrooms sizzled as he swept them into the pan.

'What's your mother like?' Aarti asked.

Euan's eyes lit up. 'People say I'm like her. She has hair as dark as yours but my eyes are like my da's. I remember when I was little, she'd take me to the beach and we'd build a big fire, toast bread curled round sticks. She'd wrap me in her blanket and we'd stay until the stars came out, watching the sea turn from bright green to indigo blue, and she'd tell me stories about the Druids and the green-blue men that swim under the waves. And she'd sing to me – there was this lullaby . . .' He trailed off and glanced down. 'Sorry, talking about her, about my family . . . it's . . .'

'You said there was a lullaby. Will you sing it to me?' Aarti suggested, stirring the mushrooms. Euan cleared his throat and, to Aarti's surprise, his voice was pure and tuneful as he started to sing . . .

'*Little youthful Blue God*
Of the fishes in the sea
If you're looking for devotion
Please choose me.'

Blue god . . . Aarti felt a shiver run down her spine. She glanced over at Euan, remembering how she had prayed for answers to her own blue god in the shrine.

Could it be a coincidence?

But Euan smiled at her, not sensing her confusion. 'Thanks, singing it does make me feel a bit better. I guess it makes me feel closer to my ma.'

'It's lovely.' Aarti tried the word on her tongue. 'Mother . . . Ma . . . Mama.' Each name felt good as her lips pressed together to make the sound that she knew she must have used before, long ago. After all these years saying it again gave her hope, even though her ma was long gone.

Euan helped her serve up the mushrooms and fried eggs, crispy round the edges. 'I'm sure your ma would have sung you lullabies too,' he said as they sat down. 'Do you remember her at all? Or your pa?'

Aarti sighed. 'Not until recently. I've always had *feelings* more than memories, like when I sleep sometimes I can sense my hand snuggled in someone else's. But over the past year, the feelings have been growing. There are smells of flowers and I'm running about in the sunshine. Sometimes I'm being held by someone. But I can never see their face; whenever I look up, everything fades and I'm back here.'

They ate in silence for a few moments, the only sound the clicks and scrapes of their knives and forks. Then Euan asked, 'Do you know how long you've been here?'

116

'All I know is that some of my clothes are really small for me, so I must have been here for a long time. Aunt said I turned twelve on my birthday this year.' Tears pricked at Aarti's eyes. 'If only I could remember more.'

'Don't cry, Aarti.'

She pushed away her empty plate and put her head on the table. Listening to Euan's stories of his family filled Aarti's mind with questions, like pebbles hitting the watery pools of her past. They sent ripples echoing into her memories and she felt a stirring, an unveiling of the darkness, voices coming forward, slowly, slowly.

The next morning it was still raining. Aarti went to the window and rubbed the pane with the cuff of her jumper. The clouds hung low and mist blanketed the walnut tree, circled the branches in the woods beyond.

She saw Euan out by the chicken coop, collecting eggs. She tapped on the window and he looked up and waved, giving her a crooked smile.

She pulled on warm trousers and socks and pattered down the stairs to the hall to check on the fire and the range, and to replace the bucket under the leak in the old storeroom, but Euan had already done it all. He'd even stacked the logs and got the porridge bubbling on the stove. She gave it a stir and poured it into bowls and took them to the table.

There was a necklace with a small spiralled shell strung on a leather lace placed beside an arrangement of small sticks laid out to spell her name: Aarti. She picked the necklace up and held it to the light, smiling.

The door opened and Euan walked in carrying the eggs in a straw basket. 'You found it?' he called as he shook off the rain, dumped the wellies and water-proof by the door and came into the hall.

Aarti felt her face redden. She tied it round her neck and felt the ridges of the shell with her finger-tips. 'This is beautiful, Euan.'

'I found the shell on the beach yesterday. I thought it would cheer you up.'

'Thank you.' Aarti smiled. 'And you made my name with sticks.' She touched the shell again. 'Thanks for making breakfast and everything. But don't overdo it, you're probably still recovering.'

'I'm good, Aarti, honest.' He put the eggs on the table and sat down, swallowing a spoonful of porridge. 'I found some rope in the woodstore. We should go and look for the cove.' Euan huffed a frus-trated sigh. 'As soon as the rain stops.'

'Great . . . though it doesn't show any sign of letting up.' Aarti and Euan both grimaced at the weather through the arched window. 'I had another of those dreams last night,' Aarti said. 'The ones like memories.'

'What happened?' Euan asked, leaning forward.

Aarti shut her eyes to conjure it again. 'I was in a garden full of flowers, but last night it was like a shadow was slowly lifting and I saw more detail than ever before. Not people, but details of things in the garden. And I felt so happy in the sunshine.'

Euan grinned, pushing the spoon into the thick, creamy porridge. 'That's great, Aarti. You're remembering more.'

'You're helping me to remember.'

16

Days went by and the rain fell without pause, slinging hard on the roof, against the windows and down the chimneys. Euan and Aarti studied the map over and over and together they prepared to find the boat.

They went to the woodstore and got the coils of rope ready, Aarti found some boots for Euan in Aunt's room and with an extra pair of socks they fitted him well, and they waited for the rain to stop.

One evening they sat by the fire warming themselves by the hot flames and Aarti showed Euan the book of folk tales all about the sea-green men. 'Look,' she said, opening the big old book *The Blue Men of the Minch*. 'It's like the little rhyme your ma used to sing you.' She showed him the page with the drawing of a ship in stormy seas and the deathly faces of blue men grasping at the sides of the boat with long tentacled fingers, pulling the sailors into the wild sea.

'We have a book like this at home . . . and this is just what we do on wet days. Sit around the fire, Ma brings out the sweet Scottish tablet and we tell stories, and as the night gets darker, the stories get scarier,' laughed Euan. A flash of lightning lit up the hall and more rain pounded on the roof.

'We tried to make tablet once,' said Aarti, 'but it didn't work so well – Aunt said we needed proper sugar.'

'We love it in our house, that butterscotch crunch – anyway, Ma has a theory; well, it's not exactly *her* theory but she really likes it. She went to a talk and a professor from some university said she'd found evidence of links between the Druids and the ancient holy men of India. Turns out they had a lot in common.'

Aarti's eyes widened. 'But aren't India and the lands of the Druids thousands of miles apart?'

'Well, that's the incredible thing – the Druids might've walked all the way to India, according to this professor.'

So they were somehow connected? The thought made Aarti's fingers tingle with excitement. 'Why don't we make something together – a painting? We can paint the blue men and Krishna and make up our own poem.'

'OK – there's not much else to do, I suppose, until the rain stops.'

Aarti fetched a huge yellowing roll of paper and spread it on the table and brought out a well-used box of paints, and they set to drawing Krishna, the Druid Amergin and the blue men.

Finally, Aarti painted a huge Chand like a red cloud floating over all of them, the crescent moon shining white on his forehead.

Under the painting, Aarti wrote a poem:

> I am the water and the oceans
> I am all the words you'll ever know
> I am every tiny sound in all the universe
> I am all the scents of summer and spring
> the earth in autumn
> and the iced air in deepest winter
> I wear the world like a jewelled cloak
> I am the beating heart of all life.

'You're good at drawing,' said Aarti, studying Euan's paintings. 'These are beautiful.'

'I like art,' said Euan. 'It's my favourite subject at school . . . You're good with words. They sound – right. It's nice to bring the two worlds together like this . . . Ma would like it.' Euan took the paintbrush, and in a corner of the painting he drew a symbol made up of three circles with three dots inside and three lines coming down from the dots. 'This is the ancient symbol of the Druids, it's called "Awen". Maybe it will bring us luck when we finally find the boat and set sail – Ma said it's the sound of the universe.'

A thud from the ceiling made them both look up and then at each other. Aarti stood quickly and crept up the stairs followed by Euan. She didn't want to go into Aunt's room but that's where the thud had come from. They stood at the door, staring in.

'The wind's blown the window open,' said Aarti, tiptoeing into the shadowy room, the wind and rain showering the floor. She leant out into the night, the rain streaming against her face, and wrestled with the catch, eventually pulling it closed with a thump.

'I think this is what made the noise,' said Euan, picking up a small wooden box from below the window ledge. He flipped it open and looked at the pale lock of hair that sat coiled inside. 'Whose hair is this?'

'Oh . . .' Aarti peered at it. 'I think it's Aunt's – or could be her mum's, I suppose.'

'Wait a second . . . Aunt was blond?'

'Yes,' Aarti said, peering over his shoulder at the curled hair. A quizzical look passed over Euan's face. 'What?' Aarti took the box from Euan and placed it on the bedside table.

'It just seems a little strange to me.' Euan studied her dark hair and brown skin. 'Are you sure she was your real aunt? You can't have looked anything alike.'

Aarti crinkled her brow in thought.

'Do you think . . . is there a chance that she was lying to you about being your aunt?'

Aarti's heart hammered against her chest.

Euan's eyes widened further. 'And if she was lying about that, what else could she be lying about? Aarti, what if your parents are still alive?'

Aarti's hands trembled. 'Do you think she would lie about something like that?' The possibility both thrilled and horrified her. But it couldn't be true, could it? Not really.

'There's no way of knowing – not until we leave. That's why we have to find the boat, Aarti,' Euan replied kindly. 'Let's head to bed and hope the storm is cleared by morning.'

Aarti lay in bed, Euan's words thundering through her mind. She pulled Squidgy close. It was true that Aunt didn't look much like her, but she always said Aarti caught the sun easily which explained their different skin. Aarti recalled the day she'd found her rabbit and asked Aunt about her past; the look on her face had been so strange – what had she been hiding?

In the middle of the night, something woke Aarti and she flicked her eyes open suddenly and couldn't get back to sleep. Maybe Euan was awake too. She went down to the hall and as her eyes adjusted to the gloom, she saw that the bundle where Euan slept was thrown aside and he wasn't there.

'Euan,' she called drowsily, but there was no answer. She rubbed sleep from her eyes and peered around the room in case he'd rolled out of the huddle during a dream, but he was nowhere in the hall.

She swallowed. Maybe all the talk of his ma and family had made him sad and he needed to get out. When Aarti felt upset, walking the island always made her feel better, so perhaps he had gone to the beach, to try to remember what happened between sailing on his boat and washing up here.

Aarti hurried into clothes and pulled on her shoes, noticing that the boots she had given to Euan were still by the door and he hadn't taken a coat or anything. She worried that he would get ill again and lifted the waterproof from the hook, folding it over her arm as she left the house.

The rain had stopped, and the dark metallic clouds hanging in the sky like a brooding presence over the island were starting to drift over, revealing the shining stars. Aarti's heart raced as she searched the walnut tree out of habit, and when she saw that the space under its low branches was empty, she again felt the sharp loss of her fox friend, like a snap to the stomach.

Throat aching, she continued along the track to the beach, hoping that Euan had only ventured this far. He still didn't know the island well – what if he stumbled in the dark, or fell down a steep bank? She should have paid more attention, told him to wake her if he felt upset; instead she had babbled on about herself, been so happy to be with someone at last that she had forgotten to think about him.

These were the thoughts that whirled through her head as she approached the beach from the direction of the standing stones, but what she saw on the darkened sand took her breath away.

17

She hid behind the tallest stone and stared down at the beach. The whole harbour was covered in a glittering veil of fine mist. The sea was frothing, the tips of the waves lifting up from the body of water to reveal slick-backed dolphins swimming and leaping in the air.

And there was Euan, standing on the beach, his flute held lightly to his lips. The most wonderful music she'd ever heard was ringing out over the bay. This music was so different to anything Aunt had played on her violin. It seemed to travel into her body and send its notes deep, where it teased the corners of her memory. He'd told her he couldn't play the flute! *What is this? What is happening? What else isn't Euan telling me?*

Even though it was night-time, there was light everywhere, the northern lights shining from the sea, from the sky, all focused on illuminating the scene. The lights spun about the sky, changing colour from blue to green, from rose to deep amber, flashing down on Euan, wrapping him in their beauty.

Euan stepped into the shallow waters and continued to play, like a welcome song for the dolphins that danced in and out of the water, in time to the tune.

The brilliant blue in the sky matched the turquoise sea and shone down on Euan, turning his skin a deep blue, shadows of fine patterns glimmering across his face and arms.

Euan paused and stopped playing, but the echo of the music still hung in the bright air.

What should she do? Should she go down to Euan, let him know that she was there and that she had seen everything? Something stopped her. It wasn't fear exactly; it was a sense that she had seen something she wasn't supposed to and it made her feel like a sneak. Maybe Euan had been coming down here every night since he arrived; with Aarti sleeping upstairs and Euan downstairs, she'd have no way of knowing.

Full of confusion, Aarti backed away, leaving Euan on the beach, bathed in the shower of shooting stars and rainbow sky, and returned to the house.

She half expected to find Euan cosied up by the fire, but his quilt was just as she had left it, gaping and empty.

She fetched her blanket from upstairs and went into the hall; she wanted to see him as soon as he came back. None of this made any sense, she thought, wrapping the blanket tight. Who was Euan really? Why had he lied to her about the flute?

In the morning, shafts of golden dust motes danced through the window and woke her. She'd meant to wait up for Euan but she must've dropped off. She hardly dared open her eyes and waited, her stomach churning, red shadows flitting on the insides of her lids, until she heard a rustling and Euan's voice bright and breezy.

'Morning, sleepyhead! What are you doing sleeping down here?'

Her eyes sprang open and she stared. He seemed exactly the same as yesterday before he had gone to sleep.

'The rain's stopped,' he said without waiting for her reply, still wrapped in his quilt. 'That means we can get on with finding the boat – at last.'

Aarti's face was still, confusion clouding her memories of what she had seen last night. She stared hard at Euan, tried to bore into him, to see if there were any clues.

'You're quiet this morning,' he said cheerfully.

She stuck out her chin and narrowed her eyes. 'I woke up in the night but you weren't here.' *Ha*, thought Aarti, as Euan's face changed.

He paused for a brief moment. 'What do you mean? I didn't go anywhere. I didn't even wake up.'

'Don't lie to me! The quilt was empty and I went to the beach. I saw it all, Euan. The sky, the sea filled with dolphins, you playing the flute that you told me you couldn't play.'

The confused expression on Euan's face appeared to be genuine – but Aarti knew what she'd seen. 'You must have been dreaming, Aarti. I swear I was here all night.' His eyes were like hollows. 'Believe me, I wouldn't lie to you. I—' He broke off, shook his head, as if he'd decided against saying whatever he was going to say.

'What is it?' Aarti wasn't going to let him get away with it.

'Look, I don't want to offend you but you have got a really vivid imagination, and . . . I can understand after everything you've been through . . .' He shuffled deeper into the quilt. 'I . . . I mean it's understandable.'

'What's understandable?'

'That you mix what's real with what's in your head. And we *have* spent days cooped up inside thinking about myths and stories, so it's not surprising.'

Aarti's heart lurched. Was he calling her a liar? 'But I saw it all, as real as day.' A sudden anger flared. 'Don't tell me I'm making it up. I saw you.'

'I believe you think you saw me. But I've been here all along, Aarti. I don't know what else to say.' Euan yawned. 'Shall we get breakfast? We need to put our efforts together to get off the island. That *is* what you want, isn't it?'

Aarti bit the inside of her cheek and let out a frustrated huff. She slammed the kettle on the stove. Grabbing hold of the oven door, she dug the spoon into the porridge she'd set to cook on a low heat the night before. A fug of hot steam hit her face and she calmed herself down. Whatever had happened last night, she'd figure it out later. Right now, Euan wasn't going to give in – and they had to work together to search the cliffs. 'What I want more than anything, Euan,' she said calmly as she lifted porridge from the oven, 'is the truth.' She brought two mugs of nettle tea and the oats and set it all down on the table. She narrowed her eyes at Euan again as he sat down. *But I will keep a close eye on you*, she thought.

After breakfast, while Euan was cleaning up, Aarti lit a candle in front of her book of the blue gods. She hoped that her wishes for finding the boat and uncovering the foggy mysteries about her past could somehow be taken like smoke from the fire up the chimney and out into the sky, up to the stars and the moon, and land in the ears of the gods who might be wandering above the clouds, or deep down in the blue-green oceans.

She darted Euan a sideways look – he was washing up the porridge pot. She could see the web of veins spread like delicate violet rivers across his lowered eyelids, his pale skin and the freckles like little islands dotted about his cheekbones.

He'd been kind to her. She touched the necklace he had given her and thought how lovely it was to have a friend at last. She didn't know what to think about his lack of explanation for the happenings of the night before. Maybe he'd been sleepwalking – though how he could have learnt to play the flute, even in his sleep, was a mystery to her. Maybe she'd make him a gift in return for her necklace, something made from the whorled walnut wood that was so pretty, because that's what friends did.

She began to hum the tune he sang about the blue gods and the fishes in the sea. Euan glanced over his shoulder at her and smiled.

18

As soon as they were ready, they set off alongside the rustling woods, the sky a pale milky blue and the ground squelchy with mud, the homemade map stored safely in the pocket of the rucksack that Aarti carried on her back.

They skirted the mountain that Aarti loved to climb, chattering between them as they went, and continued further across the rugged rocky moorland, thick with flora, like the most elaborate rug of yellows and purples you'd ever seen, their boots squishing into its luxuriant beauty.

And finally they arrived at the other side of the island, a way along from the cliffs where Aunt had scrambled down before and where she'd slipped and fallen.

They walked to the cliff edge, cheeks bright with the wind and the effort of the walk, and watched the golden eagles spiralling above them, riding the warm currents of the soft billowing breeze.

Aarti squinted into the sun-sparkled sea, avoiding looking at the rocks below where stripy beaked puffins basked. Even on this calm day the salty sea crashed against the cliffs.

She searched ahead, further along the tufted path that ran high above the sheer drop. 'Let's go down over there.'

As they approached a spot high above the rocks, they peered over the dizzying edge of the cliff. Clouds drifted over the blue sky and the sun shone silver on the choppy sea. Below her she could see a tiny curve of white beach, like a nail, hardly wide enough to walk along. The waves crashed against its edges, rushing at the sand, and the dark shadows of caves were visible beside them. Could there be a boat hidden in there somewhere?

'It's a long way down,' said Euan, 'and the sea is wild.' For the first time, he sounded afraid.

'Aunt taught me how to go down cliffs like this – she wanted me to collect eagle eggs.' Aarti dropped the rucksack at the foot of a gnarled old pine with a thick, strong trunk. 'Let's tie the rope to this tree; I know how to do the right knot. Then we'll rappel down – I'll show you how.'

'I've done it once before too with my da, but only with more than one rope and a harness. You're the expert.' Euan put his coil of rope next to the rucksack and together they secured it to the trunk.

'I'll go down first,' said Aarti, stepping into the far end of the rope and wrapping it around herself. 'You have to make a sort of harness out of the rope, with a loop here, and hold it to one side, then let it out slowly as you go down the cliff face. See?'

Once Euan had practised the movement himself, Aarti prepared to descend. 'Remember to take your time,' she said. 'Just make sure you stay horizontal all the way down. Look at the sky and push away from the rock.'

Euan nodded, his face pale but determined.

Aarti grinned. 'OK, here goes.' She backed away to the edge of the cliff and lowered herself slowly down the side of the shining rock, her face raised to the sky, her feet pushing against the cliff. Black-headed guillemots flew around her shoulders, fish dangling from their beaks as they returned to their nests tucked between the crevices of the cliff.

Her feet nudged at clusters of wild campion grow-ing out of the lichen-spotted cliff face as she fed the looped rope slowly, until she finally landed on the tiny edge of sand. She flicked a glance over her shoulder at the sea that roared and hurled itself at the rocks. She swallowed down her nerves, looked up and waved to Euan, who was standing at the top watching her.

'Your turn,' Aarti shouted.

Euan raised his thumbs and began pulling the rope up, getting himself secured into his own rope harness. He followed Aarti, copying what she had done, and slowly he lowered himself down the side of the cliff.

'Pretty good,' said Aarti, as he landed softly beside her on the beach.

'Hurts your hands a bit,' he said, getting out of the rope harness. 'But it wasn't too bad.'

They left the rope dangling and clambered on to the rocks, peering into the caves in the cliff face. The steep cliffs towered above them as they walked on until the thumbnail beach was left way behind them.

'These rocks are going on and on,' complained Aarti, trying to steady herself on their slippery surface. 'I can't imagine how Aunt would have brought a boat this way.'

'I must admit it looks unlikely.' Euan crinkled his nose. 'Shall we turn back and walk along the tops of the cliffs, see if we can find anything further down from here?'

Aarti looked thoughtful. 'Let's see what's round this corner first.'

They continued until they turned a bend and came to a wall of rock that jutted from the cliffs, creating a high barrier in front of them.

'Now what?'

'Look, there's a gap down there.' Aarti pointed to an opening at the bottom of the wall.

They crouched low, shuffled through the rock face and found themselves in a small sandy cove. The waves were much higher here, and the only way to this cove would be either by boat around the edge of the island or like they had done, using ropes. If there was a boat even Aunt would have found it hard to get to, so maybe she'd put it somewhere else after all.

They crossed the beach to the other side and entered a narrow arched sea cave, the top of which hung over the sand. Salt water ran into it from the sea. The wide stream of shallow emerald water shot into the cave and rippled against the sides of the rock, fingers of purple dulse floating under the surface.

Aarti and Euan exchanged a look of trepidation as they stepped further into the dark cave, edging along the boulders that poked out of the water, trying not to disturb the velvet crabs that skittered about in the rock pools.

Aarti noticed Euan's face lose some of its usual colour, and here in the musky darkness take on an almost blue tone, reflecting the sea water, and he slowed down a little as if he was struggling to keep up.

'Are you OK?' she asked, touching his arm.

He breathed deeply. 'Aye.'

Aarti frowned. 'Don't overdo it. Maybe we should go back?'

'I'm OK,' he grinned, straightening up, a little of the colour returning to his cheeks. 'Don't worry about me . . . let's keep searching.'

At the back of the sea cave was another cave, a dry one, where the water stopped and the sand continued to stretch further in.

Wet sand sticking to her boots, Aarti trudged ahead of Euan, entering a well of darkness and gloom, the ceiling of the second cave stretching high above them. Only a faint beam of light filtered through from above. Would Aunt really go to such lengths to hide a boat? Aarti was getting the sinking feeling there was nothing here.

Her heart suddenly rattled against her chest as she squinted into the semi-darkness, not sure what was ahead – a long boulder, or something else. Her voice came out in a strangled yelp. 'Euan, look! I think it's there!'

They both sprinted forward, towards the dark shape, and pressed their hands to the boat, hidden away at the very back of the cave.

'We found it!' they both cried, their voices rising into the dark gloom, echoing against the hard walls of rock.

'She's a real beauty,' said Euan, passing his palms across the side of the boat.

It was about five metres long, made of smooth planed wood, not too deep but rounded and wide through its middle with a small covered cabin at one end.

'She's called *Flora*,' said Aarti, tracing the faded name painted in green at the hull of the boat.

'What's this?' Aarti's fingers landed on the glint of a twelve-sided brassy coin embedded in the planks of the boat.

'1940,' read Euan. 'It's a gift from the person who made the boat. It's tradition to put a coin with the date of birth of the person who made it.'

'Maybe it was made by Aunt's mum or dad,' Aarti suggested. She lifted the cover off. Inside was a wooden mast lying flat against the bottom with sails wrapped around it.

'She's all ready to go,' said Euan.

Aarti swallowed. 'So this is the boat that carried me here.' She closed her eyes, gripped the edge of the *Flora* and tried to recall the journey. Suddenly she felt herself swaying, sea spray hitting her face, the boat bobbing up and down on the waves, and she heard sobs – squawking birds and sobs.

19

She sat down hard on a rock at the boat's side.

'Aarti?' Euan said, rushing over. 'Are you OK?'

The image of the journey to the island came back to Aarti in waves. 'It's a memory,' she said breathlessly. 'I remember holding Squidgy Rabbit, my cuddly toy, in one hand and gripping the edge of the boat with the other. And Aunt's voice, I can hear it squawking like the birds. "Stop crying," she kept saying over and over. "Stop crying." B . . . but I couldn't.'

Euan looped an arm around her shoulders and they sat quietly for a few moments. 'Aarti, this is great,' he said. 'We've found the boat now. You're one step closer to answers. And I'm closer to going home.'

'Sorry, I know this is hard for you too,' said Aarti,

wiping her cheeks, offering him a watery smile. She knew it wasn't fair on Euan. He'd been so kind to her, and all the time he must have been so upset, wondering if he'd ever see his parents again. 'Let's put the cover back and get home – it's getting late. We'll come back another time to move the boat.'

They took a final look at the *Flora* before leaving the darkened sea cave and scurried back along the boulders and through the rock pools with the crabs. 'Hurry.' Aarti balanced on the rocks and walked as quickly as she could towards the small arc of sand. 'We mustn't get trapped down here.' The sea was already beginning to hurtle into the narrowed opening of the cave, waves frothing, as they reached the foot of the cliff.

Back on the clifftop, Euan flopped on to the damp grass, unable to speak at first. 'I didn't think I'd make it,' he breathed eventually.

'It's always harder coming up,' said Aarti.

They sat looking out to sea, the late-afternoon sun glinting on its surface.

'I can't believe we've actually found it,' whispered Aarti. 'We're going to be OK, Euan. We're really going to leave.' The feeling she'd got when she touched the boat was still reeling inside her. 'It was like the boat was holding on to the memories, *my* memories of when I came here.'

'It doesn't feel like it was a happy time,' said Euan. 'If you remember crying like that and your aunt telling you to stop.'

'No,' said Aarti, her stomach knotting up. 'I don't think it was a happy time. But then, that makes sense if my parents had just died . . . assuming her story was true . . .'

'I don't know if you really can assume that,' Euan said.

The knots in Aarti's stomach pulled tighter. 'The worst thing is not knowing. I don't know if I have any family waiting for me like you do, or if what Aunt told me is true, that I don't have any family and she was the only person I had.'

They yanked up the rope from the cliff side in silence, both of them thinking about the next step. Uncertainty and fear gripped Aarti's body as she re-coiled the rope and lifted it on to her shoulder. She wasn't sure if what she had said was true: was not knowing the truth really the worst thing? Or was it worse to leave everything she had known and loved – this island, this life – to find no one waiting for her?

Well, it was too late now. She had wished for this – now she had to follow this path to the end.

The sun turned pale orange as they made their way back to the abbey, and by the time they arrived at the edge of the woods, dusk was creeping through the sky and the first stars were appearing above the chimney stacks of the house. Aarti knew she had to bury her fears and listen to Euan; she would only know everything for sure once she left the island and began to trace the truth about her past.

They creaked open the wide doors to the wood-store and hung the ropes back on the hook. Aarti collected more wood and took it inside while Euan checked on the animals.

She emptied the logs on to the stack by the side of the hearth and stoked the fires. She looked into the flames and wished they could tell her more about what she would find once she left the island. The wisps of smoke danced above the fire and curled their way up the chimney, but there was no message she could read. And now, even though some feelings had been woken up when she had touched the boat, it was like her mind was closing down and even the warmth of the sunshine in her one memory from what might be home was turning cooler. What if she'd imagined it, to comfort herself and to give herself hope? Maybe Euan was right, maybe it was all in her imagination.

'What are you thinking about?' said Euan, shutting the front door and coming to stand beside Aarti by the fire.

'Oh, nothing,' she lied. 'Just wondering what we can eat tonight. I'm starving.'

'Eggs with tatties and neeps?'

'Sounds good. We don't have to be too careful about food any more, now we know we're leaving,' she said, smiling.

Euan put two eggs on to boil and between them they began to peel potatoes and turnips, chopped them up and put them in the pan along with the eggs. Then he sat on the bench and flicked through one of the books from the shelf.

Aarti made mash and piled their plates high with the tatties and neeps, cutting them each a boiled egg, the golden yolk making a rich sauce which dribbled down the mountain of mash.

It wasn't until Aarti began tucking in to her food that she realized how hungry she was. All the thoughts racing through her mind settled and she relaxed at last.

'We'll have to make sure we pick a good day to set sail,' said Euan, scraping his plate clean. 'Summer is here but still the weather can be unreliable.'

'I think we should fetch the boat tomorrow,' said

Aarti. 'Just take it round the head of the island and bring it into the harbour. We can test it out and it will be easier to load.'

'Yes,' agreed Euan. 'We don't know yet if all the sails are still good. We need to check it over and get used to it.'

Aarti thought about leaving and a pang of guilt made her heart speed up. It was so hard not knowing what had happened to Chand.

'Are you thinking about your fox?'

Aarti nodded in surprise.

'Why did you name him Chand?'

'I – I don't know really,' said Aarti. 'There was a spot between his almond-shaped eyes like a crescent moon. When I saw it I didn't think moon straight away, I thought *Chand*, like it was the most natural thing in the world, as if he was always meant to be called Chand – it just sprang to my mind from some-where.'

Euan's eyes twinkled. 'It's a great name.'

20

The next morning, Euan knocked on Aarti's door and brought her a mug of hot tea. He placed it on the stool beside her bed and went over to the window, throwing the curtains open to a bright, sunny day.

'It's a good day for bringing the boat round,' he said.

'That's great. And thanks for the tea.' Aarti sat up in bed and sipped from the chipped mug.

Euan pushed the window open and a fresh breeze rustled into the room. It smelt of sharp sea salt and new growth. A bird settled on the window ledge and began to twitter, pecking at the insects caught in the spiderwebs.

'The swallows are here,' cried Aarti, leaping from her bed and joining Euan by the open window. 'I look forward to them coming all year – they like to nest under the eaves.' She felt excitement pulse through her like something huge was about to happen. 'Welcome back.' Aarti waved at the birds and sighed as she took in the view. 'The warm weather will be here soon – see how the woods have begun greening? In the blink of an eye it will be properly summer and we can gather the creamy mushrooms that grow under the beech trees.'

They watched the sleek-bodied swallows fly from one end of the deep-blue sky to the other, swooping and diving at full speed. Suddenly Aarti realized that she was leaving – maybe for good – and the moment was tinged with sadness. She wouldn't be able to gather mushrooms, after all. She had been so fixed on leaving the island that she hadn't thought about all the things she'd miss. Chand, the mountains, the way the island had looked after her, fed her, blanketed her over with warmth and love.

She closed her eyes and breathed in the morning air, trying to engrave this moment to her memory, so she could imagine it when she was far away.

Aarti breathed a sigh of relief when she saw the boat, same as yesterday, moored in the damp cave, the cover firmly stretched across it. She had been worried that they hadn't found it at all, that she had dreamt the whole thing.

She ran over to it and touched it lightly along its name, *Flora*.

Euan grabbed hold of one end of the boat. 'Right, let's push her to the sea.'

Aarti stood beside him and together they heaved hard, blood pumping as they shifted it out of the dry cave and towards the water.

The dry sand made a slippery surface for the underbelly of the boat to slide along and they hustled it under the arc of rock above them, closer towards the wide emerald water beyond. It wasn't far, but before long Euan stopped pushing.

'Can we take a rest?' Euan's face had taken on the blue reflection of the sea. He leant against the edge of the boat and closed his eyes.

He can't be fully better, worried Aarti, *but he doesn't want to bother me with it.* She studied his face, the dark vein throbbing on his forehead, violet bruises like petals under his long black lashes, the scatter of freckles deepening, but still he smiled, a wide calm smile.

'Are you OK?'

He opened his eyes. 'Of course. This is going to be exciting . . . that aunt of yours knew a thing about boats. It was the perfect place to store it. The wood hasn't dried out so she should be good to go.'

'I'm glad you know about boats too. I couldn't have done this without you,' Aarti said.

Once they were in the shallow water, they flipped off the canvas cover, rolled it up and stowed it in the boat then climbed in. Euan began unwrapping the sails from the mast; together they hoisted it upright.

'There are oars too,' said Euan, as they climbed back out. 'She's just about ready . . . let's push her further into the sea and then from there the tide will take us.'

Wind flapped along the white sail as they gave the *Flora* a final push into the waters.

'Get in,' yelled Euan above the noise of the seabirds, 'I'll give it one last heave and jump in after you.'

The clear water rushed at them as Aarti climbed in. She gripped the sides of the boat and the breeze smacked against the sails. She felt the boat lifting on the waves, bobbing along in the deepening sea. She watched Euan as he gave the boat one more shove and leapt in next to her, the sail making a vast triangle above their heads. He took hold of the rope attached to the sail and pulled it gently to control the wind, directing the boat away from the rocks and out along the narrow mouth of the cove.

Fulmars gathered around the *Flora* as waves lapped at her and she sailed for the first time in years, carrying Aarti and Euan away. The gentle wind buffeted the white sail, making a low murmuring sound. The boat sat low in the water, almost level with the small waves that chopped around her, and Aarti dipped her fingers in the clear green water, feeling like she was floating in the sea itself. She threw back her head and let the sun fall on her face, closed her eyes and watched the dancing red warmth spread across her eyelids.

Euan stood tall, concentrating on capturing the wind, bending the sail with the rope held tight between his fingers. 'So we'll follow the shoreline to the east and that should bring us round to the harbour?'

'Yes.' Aarti opened her eyes, scrunched them against the sun and looked up at Euan. 'Will you show me how to sail? Then we can both take turns – when we set off properly.'

'Sure. Here – we can start now.' Euan slipped the rope to Aarti. 'Tug downwards like this.' He held the rope further up and guided Aarti to move the sail so the wind was pushing it the way they wanted to go. 'OK, that's good, now just keep the pressure on. You have to tame the wind. You already know about nature and how it changes, you just need to use the power of the wind to get you where you want.'

Aarti watched Euan carefully and copied him, sailing into deeper water, further from the shore. The boat rocked and bounced, the hull cutting through the waves beautifully, and gradually Aarti got better at judging where the wind was coming from.

'You're a bit of a natural,' smiled Euan.

'It's like dancing with the wind . . . I know it sounds strange, but I used to do ballet and it's a bit like that except you have to react to what's going on around you rather than the music.'

Euan crinkled his eyes at her. 'You're a wave dancer now.'

They passed steep cliffs with golden eagles gliding down to their eyries, rocks snuggled with black-and-white puffins, their orange beaks bright against the blue sky.

'It's so different seeing the island from the sea,' said Aarti, pulling hard on the rope to guide the boat round the headland. She thought about how the island was her whole world and seemed to stretch for ever, but seeing it from the boat, she now realized how small it really was, like a pebble in a vast sea. There was so much more to discover.

*

They sailed until the sun had moved above them and continued until it began to slide towards the horizon.

'There's the top of the mountain,' cried Aarti excitedly, as the sharp peak appeared round the corner. The boat picked up speed and continued to skirt the shore. 'Not far now.' The woods appeared to their right, edging all the way to the shoreline, and next came the house with its tall chimney popping up to the sky, puffs of smoke from the fire making a welcome signal for them.

Euan tightened his grip on the rope. 'It's going to be tricky to get the boat to come in well to the harbour, so we have to really concentrate – avoid those rocks.' He nodded. 'There's deep water round there and a drag tide.'

Aarti went to the back of the boat and began moving the tiller like Euan had shown her, trying hard to steer the boat into the harbour, but as they passed the rocks the waves were suddenly fiercer than before and the boat rammed up and down. *She could do this.* Pressing her fingers so tight around the tiller they ached, she focused on guiding the boat.

The sea below churned and frothed and Aarti thought she saw something moving alongside them. She peered closer, keeping one leg pressed firm to the side of the boat. What was it? Maybe a fish with its sparkling scales, but it was too quick and went in and out of view. She really wanted to get a better look and managed to find it again, but it wasn't a fish after all – it was far too big: a seal maybe, or a dolphin swimming under the boat. She leant over the water, stretching to get a better look, and suddenly lost concentration.

She heard herself scream, tried grabbing hold of the tiller but it slipped from her grasp. Aarti felt herself lose her balance; the arc of the island swept across her vision as her body stiffened and she tumbled head first into the sea.

21

Salt water whooshed over her and filled her mouth and nostrils in huge gulps. The current whipped her body and dragged her further under the sea, the water wild and ice-cold. She sank down . . .

Had Euan even noticed she'd gone? And even if he had, how would he rescue her? She felt her heart thrum loudly in her ears as she thrashed hopelessly, the air squeezing from her lungs.

So this was how it felt to lose your breath and leave the world, tightness gripping every tiny part of you, thoughts crashing in like rocks falling from a mountain, pounding your brain while your beating heart felt further out of reach, like it belonged to someone else.

With one final effort she opened her eyes, the red sunset filtering down to where she floated under the seaweed, bubbles of light taking her off . . . drifting, drifting, down and further and all the time she heard music surround her, notes of a far-off flute.

Among the darting fish, Euan's blurry face came into view – was it Euan? His skin was bluer than turquoise, spiralled with sea shadows. Life like a spider's thread came in and out and Aarti felt a calm engulf her. They floated together, distant yet close as a dream, Euan mouthing silent words that Aarti felt glide over her.

In a sudden movement, swift and fluid as a whiplash, his arm shot out. He pulled her by the waist with a mighty strength, dragged her up, impossibly against the thickness of the briny water, swam with her to the surface and hoicked her into the boat.

Coughing out the water, Aarti emptied her lungs scratched raw by salt, the tender lining of her nose sharp with pain. The sun was disappearing and dusk settled around the bobbing boat. Beside her, Euan leant against the mast, his face changed in the low light.

'H . . . how did you do that?' spluttered Aarti.

He looked confused. 'I . . . I'm not sure. I heard a splash and couldn't see you anywhere and I didn't think, just dived in.'

'But I was so deep . . . the current was dragging me down and you – you hauled me against its force.' Given that he'd been almost too weak to push the boat to the sea, it seemed impossible.

Early moon shadows slanted across Euan's face and the gathering darkness masked his usual features.

'You. Saved. Me.' Aarti shivered, her frozen lips barely able to form the words. The warmth of the day had flown and the chill of night-time was quickly drawing in.

'Here.' Euan threw the blanket over her shoulder. 'We need to get you home.'

'But Euan . . . are *you* OK? How did you do that? You don't even look cold.'

Euan shrugged and looked away, a shadow of sadness passing over his eyes. He grabbed the rope. 'Let's go before it gets too dark to see.'

Aarti slumped against the side of the boat, her mind racing. Maybe the water had clogged her brain but there was something about Euan that made him different. She remembered the night on the beach when he had looked so strange, and just now in the blue light of dusk – it was like he was a different person, someone that she didn't know, but at the same time someone so close to her own heart he could be part of her. She couldn't explain this feeling; it didn't make any sense.

She tugged the blanket tighter, rested her chin on her knees and watched Euan with drooping eyelids as the wind pushed at the sails; the hull of the boat pointed into the harbour and the beach as he brought the *Flora* to land on the darkened sands, the waves shushing them in.

Once the water was shallow enough, Euan jumped out and brought the boat on to the dry beach. He gave her another shove, so she was solidly moored.

Silently he helped Aarti climb down from the boat, her legs wobbling as she stepped on dry ground. 'Will it be OK here?' he asked her gently.

'Yes. Th-the tide doesn't come up this far so she won't drift out.' She spoke faintly, leaning against Euan's arm.

'I'll just make sure she's protected, then we can head home,' Euan said.

Under the rising moon, Euan was full of energy, busying himself with stretching the canvas tight over the *Flora*, his cheeks alight with the effort, as Aarti shivered under her blanket on the beach.

She was exhausted; fretful butterflies zipped through her stomach as she thought how close they were to leaving. They could go any time now they'd found the boat. The *Flora* seemed ready, but was Aarti?

She gazed at the ridge of the hill, imagining Chand appearing like he used to, darting in and out of the standing stones, his ears pricked as if he had been watching for them over the sea.

'I'm going soon, Chand,' she whispered. 'But I'll never forget you.'

Her throat was tight and she was afraid to speak because if she did, she knew her words would turn to a howl.

'Come on,' said Euan. 'Let's get you warmed up.' Aarti sank her head into her shoulders and walked back beside Euan, hoping he wouldn't ask her anything, the feeling that Chand was still with her as strong as if he were actually right beside her.

Once back in the warmth of the kitchen, Euan seemed more like his usual self and Aarti felt the fire loosen the chill from her bones.

'Can we have a day tomorrow to say goodbye to the island?' she suggested suddenly. 'I haven't even shown you how beautiful it is. We could take a picnic, climb the mountain, go to the waterfall in the woods.' Ever since Euan had arrived Aarti hadn't been to the shrine and she was excited to show it to him.

'I'd like that.'

'I know how much you want to get back to your family and everything, but I promise it will only be one day and we can go after that.'

'I understand, Aarti. This is your home, even though it hasn't always been a happy place.'

Aarti felt tears wet her lashes. She pulled at the edges of her jumper – the one Aunt had given her on her special day, with the 'A' on front – as a cloud of memories swamped her.

Euan spoke again. 'This island has made you who you are – strong, clever, loving. The way I see it, that won't change when we leave. You'll carry it with you always – even when you find out the truth about your past.'

'That's what I'm afraid of – what if Aunt *was* my only family? What if this island *is* my only real home?' Aarti bit her lip. 'Euan, what do you think will happen to me when we reach the mainland – will they let me come back?'

Euan reached out and squeezed her hand. 'There will be questions, but everyone will just want to help you find the answers you need. Don't be afraid, Aarti. Look how brave you've already been.'

They cooked supper and ate it, each wrapped in their own thoughts. 'We'll have to let the chickens free and the sheep,' said Aarti.

'Yes, but they'll survive in the wild, take their chances.'

'Mmm . . . I guess.'

Later they began to gather things ready for the journey. Even though Aarti didn't have much there were some things that she wanted to take. She found the poetry book and her Krishna book, and put them on the table along with the painting and poem she and Euan had made together.

She brought down the photos of Aunt and Aunt's parents, the letters and certificates she'd found and the piece of paper that said the island belonged to her. Maybe they would help her find out the whole truth about Aunt, whether she was her aunt at all and whether it was true that she had adopted her.

Aarti stood over her pile of things on the table. She touched the seashell necklace that Euan had given her and felt its power, its whisperings from the depths of the sea.

Aarti, come home, it seemed to say.

22

That night Aarti couldn't sleep. She tossed and turned, jumbled thoughts of what lay ahead swirling around her like ghostly mist. At dawn, she threw open the windows nearly for the last time and the swallows swooped down, landing on the window ledge and wriggling into their nesting hole above Aarti's head.

'*You'll* keep coming back, won't you?' she said, tipping her head and speaking to the straight lines of the swallows' tails that poked out of the nest.

It was going to be another beautiful day. Across the woods the leaves were getting broader and the branches were alive with busy rustling. The soft wind shook the dew from the grasses and the scent of wildflowers woke and rose into the cool summer air. Aarti remembered how it had been before Aunt died – how trapped she'd felt, how alone when Aunt was in a bad way. Things were different now, but those feelings would always remain, buried deep inside.

She breathed in. She could hear Aunt's voice now – *I brought you here when nobody wanted you.* And now Aarti was running away. *Ungrateful girl.*

She let out a long breath and pushed Aunt's voice to the back of her mind. She would enjoy her final day on the island. On *her* island, she thought fiercely. Maybe one day she could come back, because despite everything it had been like a mother to her, had given her so much and had healed her aching heart when Aunt had been cruel.

Aarti left the window open and picked Squidgy Rabbit off her bed. The brooch Aunt had given her sparkled and Aarti felt herself soften. Squidgy wasn't so dirty any more and she pushed his little face closer. There was a faint scent she could smell when she first woke up, deep in his fur. It wasn't the musty house smell or the fresh island smell; it was a fragrance of roses.

'Aarti,' came Euan's voice from the foot of the stairs. 'Breakfast!'

She smiled, placed Squidgy on her pillow and hurried downstairs.

'What am I going to do when I don't have you around?' she asked Euan, only half joking.

'You'll be fine. You can come and visit, any time. My ma will love you.'

They walked into the hall. 'Even in this short time, I feel like I've known you for ever, like you're the brother I never had.'

'I'm good at being a brother – and you're good at being a sister. That's what siblings do, take care of each other.'

Sizzling on the griddle was a pile of potato cakes – the oats in the glass jar had finally run out. 'I collected eggs already,' he said, flipping the browned cakes on to two plates. 'And I made extras so we can take them on the picnic.'

'Let's boil them to take along. We'll get hungry,' said Aarti, setting a pan of water on the range and slipping four eggs in.

They guzzled the breakfast down in big mouthfuls, full of excitement for the day ahead, and packed everything they needed into a rucksack.

'I want to show you the waterfall,' said Aarti, closing the front door behind them. 'It's in the woods. And there's something special there I want you to see.'

A swirling feeling that began in the pit of Aarti's stomach uncurled itself and spread unexpectedly through her body and made her clench her fists. This could be the final time that she would walk the island. She knew it so well, every curve of beach, each tree in the woods, where the shelters were. Euan was right; for good or bad she was part of the island and the island was a part of her. How would she survive without it?

She shook the thoughts from her mind and led Euan into the canopy of fresh green trees, alive with the chatter of birds busy with their nest-making. They fell into a silence marked by the swishing sound of their feet against the forest floor. Aarti was collecting her memories, tucking them safely away so she would never forget.

A deer darted boldly across their path and sprinted away uphill, treading delicately between the green shoots of wild garlic.

'That's one of my favourite smells,' said Aarti, bending low to pull a bunch. 'We can have some with our potato cakes.' Its pungent scent filled the air. 'A sign that summer is here.'

Euan breathed deeply too, the gentle breeze blowing his dark hair about his shoulders. 'Mmmm . . . Ma makes the best sauce with wild garlic, every year.'

They carried on through the woods until the river widened, brown with peat off the hills, and they followed it along until they came upon the enchanted glade, the dip in the landscape where high boulders covered in bright green moss made a narrow opening and the river shot through it.

'Up here,' panted Aarti, edging alongside the rushing river, slippery with rocks. She paused. 'There! Isn't that the most beautiful thing you've ever seen?'

The boulders became huge through the opening, and from high above their heads the waterfall cascaded like a river creature, smooth and clear, diving down the wooded valley. Water mist rose off its back and filled the air with a damp sparkle that caught in the shaft of yellow sun trickling through the trees.

'This is my magic spot,' said Aarti, looking closely at Euan.

'It's incredible.' He stared at the waterfall gushing into the river.

'Shall we swim?' asked Aarti.

They dived into the cold river, Aarti pushing herself to its dark depths, spreading her fingers wide, paddling as freely as an otter. 'Over here,' she said, hauling herself out of the pool, leading Euan carefully to the ledge behind the waterfall. 'Isn't this amazing?'

They sat on the mossy rock to catch their breath, dangling their feet above the river, the slick water making a shield before them. 'When I couldn't take any more of Aunt, this is where I used to come – she'd never find me here.' Aarti dried herself and offered the towel to Euan.

'Your own secret haven.'

'And this isn't even the best bit,' Aarti said. 'Come and see.'

Euan followed Aarti into the cave behind the waterfall.

'It's like this ledge was made for a shrine,' said Aarti, showing Euan the objects she'd collected over time from all across the island. 'Chand led me here and later I brought my Krishna book. I'd make wishes here. For help. For answers.' She smiled. 'And see? Now you're here and we're leaving, it's like they've been answered.'

'It's really tranquil,' he said, examining the things on Aarti's shrine. 'Will you bring these things along when we leave?'

Aarti considered this for a moment but shook her head. 'I'm going to leave everything just how it is.' She stepped towards the entrance, stood for the last time staring out at the waterfall.

'You didn't tell me about this,' called Euan.

'About what?' Aarti walked back into the cave and stood beside him.

He was squinting at something on the wall behind the shrine, pulling at the moss that had grown over it. 'It's the Awen symbol I told you about.'

'That's strange . . . I've been here so many times, but I've never noticed that before.'

'Maybe it was always a shrine.' Euan carried on yanking at the moss. 'It's been hidden here for years.'

Aarti could see the symbol now. It was carved deeply into the rock, pockmarked by yellow lichen, the same three circles surrounding the three dots and the thick lines making points that Euan had drawn on their painting.

'Do you think this is a Druid island?' asked Aarti. She swallowed as she remembered the night on the beach, how different and strange Euan had appeared – and yesterday, when he had pulled her from the water with superhuman strength. She still couldn't figure out what was going on with him.

'I think there's something special about this island – the standing stones mean that thousands of years ago it was important enough to have the circle built here.'

She stepped towards Euan, close enough to look into his eyes, dark brown flecked with gold. 'It's a bit strange that you found the symbol, even though it was covered by layers of moss.'

He turned away.

Aarti felt the carving with her palm and thought about the sound *Awen*, wrinkled her forehead in thought and tried to imagine the person who had carved it.

By the time they made their way home after their farewell picnic, the light was beginning to fade. The sky had turned indigo, slashed orange across the horizon, and the moon had risen, a swollen globe over the woods.

'One final stop,' said Aarti as they approached the standing stones above the harbour. She thought about the Awen symbol behind the shrine in the cave. She placed her palms flat on the solid surface of the stones and stared up at the stars that were appearing like glints of glass, making an arc above her, and she thought that wherever she went from here these stars would always be constant; they would follow her and she could look up and find comfort there.

'People would have hauled these stones for miles,' said Euan, pressing his back against one. 'Can you even imagine how they did that?'

'They would have brought them over the sea,' murmured Aarti.

'Magical stones.'

A bat, quick as a heart-flutter, skimmed Euan's head and disappeared into the dusk. Aarti remembered the night she had stood here and discovered his body washed up on the tide, how she had seen the strange tattoos etched across his blue face and had thought she had found some creature from myth. And then it turned out he was this boy, this kind boy who had come to take her away and find her family – if she had one.

Aarti slipped her hand into her pocket. 'I made this for you.' It was a carving the size of her little finger, a porpoise with a small hole through its back where she'd threaded a piece of string. 'Dunter.' She smiled shyly. 'It's for you so you don't forget me once you get to your family. And you can show it to them, in case they don't believe that we met on this island that we can't find on any maps.'

'It's beautiful. Look at the swirls of the walnut wood – precious.' He tied it around his neck where it hung above the silver flute – which, although he claimed not to play, he never removed. 'Thank you, Aarti.'

And they walked home deep in thought, the night falling around them, preparing themselves for tomorrow, the day they would leave for ever.

23

The next morning, they saw to the chickens and sheep and made sure they could run free. 'Please Chand,' whispered Aarti, 'wherever you are, will you protect the chickens? Make sure the other foxes leave them alone?'

Aarti stood at the front door and took one final look through to the hall, her chest swarming with confusion.

Aunt's voice came echoing through the house as if she were still inside, calling to her, the kind voice as well as the stern one. Aarti felt self-conscious, like there were eyes on her. She turned swiftly, the hairs on the back of her neck bristling, and left the house.

Euan was a few paces ahead, already eager to reach the sea. When they arrived at the harbour they found the *Flora* waiting for them and hurriedly assembled everything into the small cabin.

'It's all looking good,' said Euan, completing the last checks on the boat. 'We can push her out and the tide will take us away.'

Aarti's stomach stabbed with a sudden panic, but she shoved it away and gripped the edge of the cover, stowing it under the seats. Euan hoisted the sail and the *Flora* glided into the shallow waters. Aarti was leaving the island.

She flicked her gaze back to the hill above the harbour and imagined she saw her fox between the standing stones. 'I'll always love you, dear Chand,' she said.

In the distance, white puffy clouds rose up between the patches of soft blue sky and the water, clear mint-green, lapped below them. Euan took the rope and caught the wind, which billowed the sail, cracking against the fabric.

Aarti watched the island become smaller as the wind drove them into the vast emptiness of the sea, until it was only a smudge far away and the next time she looked, her heart fluttered because she couldn't see it at all.

'Do you want to take over?' Euan handed Aarti the rope and they swapped places. 'Are you OK?'

'Mmm – just thinking of what lies ahead, how long before we see land, what happens next.'

'If only we could predict the future.'

'I bet you can't wait to see your ma and da, your little sister.'

His dark eyes glistened. 'Aye . . . it feels like so long ago that I saw them.'

Aarti tugged at the sail, turning it to capture the breeze. 'I expect they'll have been looking for you.'

'My da for sure, with others from the village . . . Ma at home, frantic. She'll be knitting something – that's what she does when she's worried, knitting me a scarf or something . . . getting longer and longer.'

Aarti could see the thought upset him and she started to sing the lullaby he'd taught her, softly.

When she was finished, Euan reached over and squeezed her hand. 'Thanks, Aarti.'

'Let's get our painting out and wish for a safe voyage for both of us,' she suggested.

Euan fished into the rucksack and brought out the roll of painting they had created together and the lines of poetry written in Aarti's curled, old-fashioned writing.

'You can leave the rope tied up just there,' said Euan. 'The wind is even, we'll just keep bobbing on.'

Aarti slid in beside Euan. 'I love the way we've got all these blue gods together. Krishna, your blue men of the sea and the Druid Amergin. I wonder if they're the same?'

'Maybe . . . Everything is connected, after all.'

Aarti held the shell necklace and wished for safe passage. She felt the rocking of the boat and all around her the blue sea draped like a piece of ruffled silk going on for ever and beyond.

'Blue gods, take us across your blue seas to land and safety – to Euan's family who are waiting and to my future, whatever it holds.'

Sea spray showered them in drops of glimmering water and the *Flora* cut through the waves, onwards and onwards through the rest of the day and towards the inky night.

24

At sunset, stars like handfuls of scattered diamonds flashed above them, blinking in and out of the gathering clouds, watching over Aarti and Euan as they sailed further and further away from the island. The white sail flapped against the darkening sky, like the wings of a giant seabird.

'Shouldn't we have reached land by now?' Aarti said, breaking a long silence.

'I'd have thought so. We've been heading south,' Euan said. 'I didn't think your island could be all this far from land. I couldn't have drifted days . . . could I? But I don't think there are any islands more than a day's sailing from the mainland. We'll be reaching home soon, I'm sure.'

Aarti yawned, pulled at the rope as Euan had taught her, and fixed the sail. She looked over the side of the boat, the dark water mysteriously churning around her, careful not to lean too far. The boat sat so low in the sea that she felt a part of it, as if they were a tiny sea creature skimming under a silver moon. Salty, damp breath rose around them and settled on her skin, making her shiver.

'I don't like the look of those clouds,' Euan said, frowning into the dimly glowing horizon. Aarti gazed up. He was right: dark clouds were gathering overhead, low and threatening.

'It's strange that I never saw a boat in all the time I lived on the island, not even when I looked from high up on the mountain.' Aarti frowned. 'But Aunt couldn't have sailed and sailed for days and nights – just her with me bawling and sobbing. You're right; we can't be far now.' The memory of coming to the island for the first time was suddenly so sharp it took Aarti by surprise and she closed her eyes. It was like she was watching herself, little Aarti, from the dark sky, and there was Aunt fixed on navigating the boat, ignoring her wailing that bleated on and on.

She and Euan hadn't planned for this long at sea – they'd packed enough for the day and a little extra. If they didn't find land soon, their food supplies would run low and they'd have to save on water. Aarti peered anxiously at the clumps of clouds, but even as she watched, the wind blew them into dark shapes that morphed and merged with one another, making ever bigger monster clouds. The boat rocked from side to side and jolted up and down. Fat drops of cold rain began to fall, slowly at first then faster.

Euan stood at the mast, his jaw tense, his fingers gripped tight around the rope, tugging at the sail. 'Storm,' he shouted above the sudden whipping sound of the wind. Waves splashed into the boat. 'We'll have to put the sail down and let her float.'

'Should we ride it out in the cabin?' Aarti yelled back.

Euan nodded, looking out across the steel-dark waters, rain grazing his skin before it turned sudden and sharp, showering them from all directions.

They struggled to fold the sail around the mast, but the wind snatched it from their grip, the waves rocking and tilting the boat, sending them tumbling against the sides.

Aarti grabbed for the sail, everything blurred by the rain. 'I've got it,' she cried, her fingers numb and slow to bend, but then it crashed away, like a serpent flailing in the air, the wind raging at it.

The frenzied storm clawed its dark shadow over them, blasted them with sheets of solid rain as they tried desperately to control the sail between them, back and forth until at last together they wrapped and twisted the rope tight and knotted it safely. Lowering the mast so it lay flat along the boat, they swayed their way to the shelter of the cabin.

The rain pounded the narrow windows as the storm whirled around the boat like a demon, tossing and swinging it as if it were made of paper. Aarti's stomach tightened and she pressed her arms around herself, pulling her knees to her chin, blood draining from her face.

She looked out at the roaring, screaming storm, at the waves that rose high above the *Flora* and bashed down on her, again and again, at the sky deafened by noise and hard, biting rain. She noticed Euan staring into the storm, his eyes wide. 'I know you're thinking of the *Dunter*,' she whispered.

'How it smashed to pieces in the storm, you mean?' His voice was hollow, desperate. A cold fear crept into Aarti's heart and sat there like a shard of ice, but she tried to push it away and moved closer to Euan. 'Don't.'

But he carried on. 'I thought I could help you, but all I've done is drive us into the arms of this storm.' He touched the carved dolphin that hung from the leather cord and sat in the small hollow at the base of his throat. 'Maybe the blue gods *are* swimming out there in the dark sea, under the boat, pulling it down.'

Aarti remembered a story he'd told her round the fire. 'Are you thinking of the tale you told me – of fishermen caught out in a storm worse than this one?' she said softly. 'Because I don't think you sh—'

But he cut her off, looking past her, his eyes unfocused. '*The thing they dragged up from the waves was huge and wild and they looked at it in horror*,' Euan recited, his voice flat and cold. Aarti shrank away from him, suddenly frightened of how the lightning sent dark blue patterns dancing across his skin. Like the night she'd found him.

'*They didn't know where it had come from or what it was*,' he continued. '*And they hurled it back into the roiling waves, fiercer than a sea monster with its gnashing jaws.*'

'Stop!' yelled Aarti, grabbing him by the arm. 'Euan, stop it.'

He jolted and at last seemed to see Aarti beside him. 'I – I'm sorry,' he murmured.

'It's OK,' whispered Aarti in relief as Euan appeared to return to himself. She stared at his pale face, his eyes swept with horror. She wiped at Euan's cheek with the damp cuff of her jumper. Then she lifted her head and peered out of the window, the rain still sputtering on the dirty glass, the storm metallic and hungry and grey.

They slid through the dense rain, Aarti whispering the poem she had written to go with Euan's painting, as if it were a prayer. If she'd had fire, and if it had been safe, she would have lit a candle, a ray of hope to get them through the storm, get Euan back to his family.

She sang the words from the poem.

'*I am the water and the oceans*
I am all the words you'll ever know
I am every tiny sound in all the universe
I am all the scents of summer and spring
the earth in autumn
and the iced air in deepest winter
I wear the world like a jewelled cloak
I am the beating heart of all life.'

Still the storm thundered, lightning searing the darkness.

'Remember that night on the island?' Euan's voice was dreamy, different again to his usual way of speaking. 'When you followed me to the beach?'

'You mean when you told me I didn't know the difference between what was real and what was in my imagination?' She felt the hurt again.

His face was shadowed, mottled blue in the semi-darkness. 'The truth is, I came to the island to fetch you.'

'What are you talking about? You're not making any sense.'

'You called me, and I came because you are good and kind and brave.'

She didn't know what to say and shrugged, swiped at the tear that sneaked from the corner of her eye. 'I don't understand,' she said quietly.

'You see,' he began again in that strange voice that seemed other-worldly. 'We are connected. I have always been in your heart.' He lifted the flute from his neck and began to play.

Fear stabbed at Aarti's insides. She remembered the night on the beach – how he'd insisted the next morning it had never happened, that he couldn't play the flute at all. What if he hadn't been lying? What if he really didn't remember it? What if, when he played the flute, he wasn't Euan at all but someone else? Some*thing* else. She still couldn't wrap her head around how he had managed to rescue her when she'd fallen in the ocean, the strength she'd felt as he pulled her to the surface.

The boat jolted violently and he stopped playing all of a sudden, leaving a blue mark on his lips where the instrument had pressed firm.

Aarti clasped his clammy hand as the frantic waves bombed the window. 'Euan, what's happening to you?' But Euan didn't reply.

She stared hard out the window. Through the beating rain she thought she saw something, a blurred smudge of light a way away, appearing and disappearing. The fuzzy light filled the cabin, like fog, and for a moment she couldn't see Euan; she felt as if she were alone. The boat tipped scarily to one side, filling with water. Her chest tightened. *Are we going to sink?*

Euan's voice floated in the radiance. 'It was your imagination that kept you going and gave you hope.' He was speaking again in his strange, dreamy voice. 'You are strong – you have everything inside yourself to take you forward.'

She knelt on the wooden bench and put her face close to the window, rubbed at the pane steamy with breath.

'Euan,' she cried, her voice trembling, 'there's something out there.'

25

Euan knelt beside her and strained his eyes through the rain-veiled sky to where Aarti pointed. He let the strangled breath loose and allowed himself to uncurl his fists. 'It's a boat,' he shouted. 'A boat!' And to Aarti's relief, his voice was once again his own.

'But how will they see us through the storm?'

'They'll have equipment that'll tell them we're here, even if they don't see us.'

Aarti grabbed hold of Euan's hand. It felt warm and real, and he squeezed back. 'I thought for a minute that you weren't here.' She felt her heart quicken. No wonder she was feeling strange, not sure what was real or not. It was all taking its toll: the storm, the tiredness and lack of sleep, the years with Aunt on the island. Maybe Euan had been right before – maybe it was all in her head.

Kneeling side by side on the bench, they watched the light make its way closer to them through the whirling mist and wind.

The low sound of a foghorn came like a seal song, and they saw the blurred outline of a large grey boat appear alongside them.

Out in the storm that still lashed the sea with its pounding force, a row of faces appeared on the boat; their mouths opened and closed as they called to them through the rain.

Aarti stood up, her legs wobbling. Her hands shook as she grabbed at the rucksack. She hugged Euan. 'Thank you for saving me.'

'We saved each other,' he said, smiling and shuffling away awkwardly.

They slid the cabin door open and staggered out to the deck, wading through the salt water, gripping the sides of the boat as it tipped to and fro on the waves.

'We'll come alongside,' came the voice faint through the wind.

The rain pelted Aarti so hard that she could barely see, but she curled her fingers over the edge of the boat to steady herself, the voices drifting closer.

'We're going to put the gangplank across,' called the voice. 'And we'll come over to get you.'

A man with a greying beard, dressed head to foot in bright yellow waterproofs, appeared through the rain, held his arms out towards Aarti. 'Don't be scared, you're safe now, take it steady and hold my hands.'

Aarti brushed rain from her eyes and took hold of the man's big rough hands, and he lifted her on to the wooden bridge they had hooked across. She crawled forward unsteadily, the man guiding her and backing away until they were on the other boat where another man lifted her off and down.

'My friend,' said Aarti. 'He's just behind me.'

The first man looked confused. 'There's no one behind you,' he said. 'There's no one but you on that wee little boat . . . all alone in this wild storm. What were you thinking, lassie?'

Fear ripped through Aarti. 'No – it's Euan, he's there. We were together.' She leant against the rescue boat and called out, 'Euan!'

She saw him still standing in the boat, his face like it had appeared on the first night she'd found him, shadowed with inky blue tattoos, flitting across him, his dark eyes looking back at her.

'Euan, what's wrong? Just come up on to the boat. Why aren't you coming?'

The wind battered him, as if it were smudging

him out; the rain swirled around him, but he didn't move, just raised his flute to his lips and played that haunting tune.

The man with the greying beard took Aarti gently by the shoulders, stared out to the *Flora* to the exact spot where she could see Euan. 'There's no one there.'

'Get the wee thing in here before she freezes,' came another voice from inside the cabin and they shuffled her away from the storm-drenched deck.

Aarti was numb, her heart racing, thumping hard against her ribs. What was happening? Why didn't they see Euan? Tears dripped down her already soaked face and she shook the men off, rushed back outside to the deck and stared back at the *Flora*.

'Euan!' she yelled. 'Come on! What about your ma and da and your wee sister, they're waiting for you!' All she could hear was the tune of his flute still haunting the storm, lifting up and away with the wind. He was still there, shadows flitting across him, the rain-mist swirling around him, dark sea lapping at his body.

When she blinked again he was gone.

'Euaaaan!'

Aarti tried to leap from the boat, but the men held tight and bundled her inside. She began to shut off, retreated inside herself, her head filling with noise and brightness and voices. It all pumped around her like a raucous thunderclap, making her dizzy and sick.

'You could have been out there for days,' said the man with the greying beard who watched over her. 'Lucky we came this way and saw you on our radar . . . we'll bring your wee boat in too.'

The voices rumbled on in the background like the rush of the sea. Aarti heard snatches of what they were saying – *Police, Authorities* – but she couldn't make sense of anything. Her fingers found the shell that Euan had given her, and she could feel its solid ridges sharp against her skin.

Euan had never told her exactly where he was from, so how could she even find his home and tell his family what had happened, that he loved them and thought about them every day and was trying to get back to them?

Why hadn't he come?

The tune from Euan's flute floated about in her head and lulled her to sleep as confused tears slipped down her cheeks.

Aarti opened her eyes slowly, felt her head throbbing and her mind filled with so many mixed-up thoughts she couldn't work anything out. *Where was she? What had happened? Where was Euan?* She felt the edge of a blanket and the hard makeshift bed beneath her. She tried to get up, but gentle big hands coaxed her back.

Drip by drip she remembered it all. The storm had blown away and now she peeped blue sky streaming in through the tops of the window in the small cabin where she lay. Around her were four men dressed in yellow waterproofs, busying themselves with the workings of the boat.

One of them looked over. 'Woken up, have you, wee one?' He stirred hot water into a mug and held the steaming drink towards her. 'I'm Jim . . . we rescued you.'

She pulled Squidgy Rabbit from the rucksack and held him close, took the tea with the other shaky hand and sat up, words snagging her throat.

'We've called ahead to shore so once we get there, we'll work things out . . . don't worry, we'll sort things. And you can tell us everything.' Jim touched Aarti's cheek lightly. 'I've a granddaughter your age.'

Aarti felt more lost than ever. She didn't know anything, what was real, who she was, what had happened to Euan – nothing.

26

Aarti lay still in the bed in the cabin, her eyes closed against the world, the knot sitting cold in the pit of her stomach like a heavy stone. She tightened her fingers around Squidgy's soft body and let the men's voices murmur about her. How was she going to tell them about the island and Aunt when they didn't believe that Euan was on the *Flora* too? She felt the sway and shift of the boat as it continued towards its destination, drifting in and out of slumber.

The foghorn woke Aarti and she crunched open her salt-crusted eyes sticky with sleep. The too-loud squawking of seabirds filtered in through the open cabin door. Her throat ached with the loss of Euan, her first and only human friend.

'We're here,' said Jim, kneeling down beside the bed. 'Your family will be mad with worry, so as soon as we anchor we'll call them. We sent a message

190

ahead to the coastguard.' He pointed at the toy. 'Who's this wee fella?'

'I . . . it's my Squidgy Rabbit,' croaked Aarti, stiffening. How did she know these were good people, that they wouldn't be mean?

'And you,' he said gently. 'What's *your* name?'

'Aarti,' she whispered, her heart thumping. 'Aarti Macdonald.'

'OK, Aarti Macdonald, let's get you to shore.' He scooped her up. 'It's OK, hen,' he soothed, as he took her off the boat. 'We'll not hurt you.'

Outside, purple clouds streaked across a pale blue sky, the tip of a setting sun hurrying towards the horizon.

She looked over Jim's shoulder, strained her eyes to the *Flora*, which was secured behind the bigger boat, but it was eerily empty. *What happened to you, Euan?*

Jim took her into a building and put her down on a chair. 'I'll call my cousin. He's a police sergeant in the next village, he'll get the ball rolling.'

A woman with rosy-red cheeks hurried through the door.

'Beth, love,' said Jim. 'This is Aarti Macdonald and she needs some looking after.'

Aarti grasped Jim's arm, her eyes wide with shock and fear. 'What about Euan? He must be out there still . . . maybe he fell into the water – can you go back and look, *please*.'

'We already radioed out, hen, but I'll check again and we'll keep looking.' He disappeared into the coastguard's office where the other fishermen were gathered.

'Don't be scared,' said Beth, taking Aarti's hand. 'I'm Jim's wife. They *will* keep looking for your friend, I promise.'

A scent of soap hit Aarti's nose, reminded her of the hidden smell of roses buried deep in Squidgy Rabbit's fur.

'Can you walk?'

Aarti nodded, stood up shakily and let herself be led outside. In the harbour, the rescue boat was moored beside half a dozen smaller boats that bobbed on the waves, and Aarti looked for the final time at the *Flora*, her stomach folding in on itself as she felt the loss of her friend again.

Orange street lights popped on and Aarti shielded her eyes at their strange brightness. They walked along the seafront, past a huddle of houses, and opened the gate to a cottage standing in a small garden. Beth turned the handle and they went inside.

'Come in, lassie,' said Beth, walking ahead into the warm kitchen, where a pot hissed on the stove and a dog snoozed in a basket by the range. He lifted his head and winked open an eye before going back to sleep. 'Sit yourself down here.' She showed Aarti a big comfy armchair.

'Now.' She cupped Aarti's tiny hands between her own and examined her closely. 'I'll need to check you over,' she said. 'I'm a nurse, do you understand? I look after people when they're ill. And we'll need to call your family. We don't understand how you were so far off land, all alone in that sailing boat . . . and you look as if you haven't eaten for a year, and ach, look at your wee face and hands.' Her eyes glistened. 'I'll run you a hot bath and after I'll see that you're not hurt, OK?'

Aarti looked at her fingernails rimmed with mud, at the scratches and cuts on her hands from all the rough work they had always done, and at Beth's hands, smooth and soft, her clean pink nails so different to her own. She stared at Beth, her mouth clamped shut, thoughts crowding her mind.

'Don't try to speak . . . you've had a huge shock.'

Beth took her upstairs and prepared a bubbly bath like the ones Aarti had read about in storybooks back on the island. She stood with her back pressed against the bathroom door, feeling out of control, so out of place she didn't know how to behave. She watched Beth from under her lashes.

'It's just a bath,' began Beth as she knelt beside Aarti. She studied her face quietly, her eyes searching Aarti's, trying to grasp who she was. She eventually gave a deep sigh as if something had clicked and she realized that Aarti hadn't just been lost at sea for a few days, that there was much more to her story. 'Have you had a bath before?'

'No,' murmured Aarti.

'You can lock the door like this,' she said softly, 'and put your clothes here – it's OK, I'll be downstairs if you need me.' Beth smiled and left, closing the door gently.

Aarti was still unsure about everything, but thanks to Euan, she recognized kindness. Once in the bath, she allowed herself to unknot her limbs, sank into its heat and scent, dunked under while the years of mud and dirt fell from her hair and slipped from her skin. Aunt had taught Aarti to wash with a chopped-up scratchy towel, and when she remembered she would heat water in the kettle to wash Aarti's hair.

She didn't understand anything. Where was Euan? Had she made him up? Had she really been alone on the boat? Fear raced through her like fire – what would happen to her now? She didn't understand this world that was so full of noise and smells, hard glare and people that made her want to bury herself under dark blankets. She should have stayed on the island. She sank to the bottom of the bath, curled herself tight like a shell – why couldn't she disappear like Euan did?

If you're looking for devotion, please choose me – the lullaby Euan sang bubbled in her ears as she gasped for breath. When the water had grown cold and she couldn't stay in the bath any longer, she hauled herself out and watched the water swirl out and down the plughole. She imagined all the years of misery with Aunt flushing away, like the dirt and mud from her body.

Aarti dried herself, pulled on the pyjamas that Beth had left on the chair and nervously walked down the carpeted stairs.

'In here,' called Beth from the kitchen. She brought a bowl of steaming soup and bread and offered it to Aarti on a tray. 'You get yourself cosy in there and get this down,' she said too cheerily.

Aarti collapsed into the big armchair, covered herself with the blanket that Beth gave her and set the tray on her lap. She blew on the hot soup and with each mouthful began to feel its warmth soak into her body, down her throat, to her stomach and right to the tips of her toes.

The dog sidled over and sat by her feet.

'This is Skye, he likes you.'

Aarti pushed her feet into Skye's long dark fur. She ate the soup and Beth busied herself in the kitchen, chopping vegetables, stirring the pot and writing something in a notebook. 'I put your clothes in the machine – I'm sorry, but the jumper's ruined by the storm, I'm afraid.'

The pretty jumper that Aunt gave me. Aarti felt a twinge of sadness. She loved the jumper and it reminded her that Aunt *was* kind sometimes.

A sudden ring jolted Aarti and filled her with panic. Beth quickly picked up the phone. She nodded and looked in Aarti's direction and then put the phone down. 'Signal's terrible up here,' she said. 'We have to have a landline.'

Aarti looked at her blankly. What did she mean by a landline?

Beth pulled up a chair and brought it close to her. 'Do you have a phone?'

Aarti didn't understand what she wanted and felt her brow crease in confusion. Although there wasn't one at the abbey, she'd read about phones, but they weren't the sort of thing you could carry around. How could she have one with her?

'Or perhaps your parents' number? We need to call them, let them know you're safe.'

'I . . . I don't know about my parents,' stuttered Aarti. 'I lived on an island with my aunt. After my parents died in an accident, she adopted me . . . there wasn't anyone else there.'

Beth's eyes widened and she held Aarti's hands again. 'What happened to your aunt?'

'She fell off the cliff. I was completely alone . . . until Euan came.'

'What was this island called?'

'I . . . I don't know.' Tears were streaming down Aarti's face, though she didn't know why. She wiped her cheeks. 'Sorry.'

'Crying is normal, after what you've been through.' She squeezed Aarti's hands. 'I'm going to make sure you're not hurt, OK?' She went to a cupboard and brought out a bag. 'Try to relax, I'll be gentle.' Beth checked Aarti's temperature, her reflexes, looked into her eyes with a small bright torch. She rolled Aarti's sleeves up and smoothed her fingers along Aarti's thin arms, pressing lightly.

'The miracle is that you're fine,' she smiled. 'How old are you, Aarti?'

She bit the inside of her mouth. 'Aunt said I was twelve.'

'You've done really well,' said Beth, stroking Aarti's cheek. She put the bag away. 'Up to bed now.'

27

'Euan!' Aarti woke, covered in sweat, screaming his name.

She heard Beth's voice, as if it were swimming through seaweed. 'It's OK,' she breathed. 'It's over, you're safe.'

Aarti pushed the covers away and felt her heart pulsing, her body trembling.

Beth put her arms around her and drew her close. 'Shhh,' she whispered. 'Hush now.'

Slowly, the dream shook itself away – she wasn't on the boat any more and Euan had gone, she had to understand that. She couldn't explain it, but his words rang in her mind: *you are strong – you have everything inside yourself to take you forward.* That's what he'd said during the storm when he had seemed less like the Euan she knew on the island and more like someone else.

'Tell me about Euan,' said Beth kindly.

Aarti didn't know if she should try to explain again. What if Beth didn't believe her either and thought she was making everything up?

'Here, have a drink.' Beth helped Aarti to sit up and held a cool glass of water to her lips.

She felt the cold water unstick her dry mouth and she gulped it down. 'Thank you.'

'So who is Euan?'

'He was my friend,' she began quietly. The bedroom was lit by a small lamp that cast its warm light across Aarti's face. 'My only friend. I lived alone with Aunt almost all my life and I only had Chand before Euan. He was a fox – but then he left me too.'

Beth didn't interrupt Aarti or ask any questions; she let her speak slowly and at her own pace.

'Euan was injured,' continued Aarti. 'He'd sailed out in a storm, he said, and his boat had capsized. He washed up on the tide and I brought him back to health and he helped me get away from the island. He made me realize that maybe Aunt had been lying all along. Maybe she wasn't even my aunt. Do you think my parents could be alive?' Tears pooled in Aarti's eyes and it felt like brambles were clawing at her throat.

'Oh, hen . . . was she a kind aunt?'

'She could be. When I was smaller, especially. But lately . . .' She shook her head.

'And you left the island with Euan?'

'Yes . . . we found a boat hidden in a cave. It must've been the one Aunt used to bring me to the island. But I don't know why he wasn't on the boat when we were rescued. I could see him, but Jim couldn't.'

'He meant a lot to you, your friend Euan, I can tell.'

'He was very kind and clever, a . . . and he made me feel like I could do anything if I wanted to. He told me about his family.' Aarti leant down from the bed and delved into her rucksack. 'We made this together.' She unrolled the picture of Krishna and the blue gods and Amergin. 'He loved art. He said it was his favourite subject at school.'

Beth looked down at the paintings and the words of the poem. 'The ancient Scottish myths, and maybe from your heritage too? Woven together.'

'The thing is,' said Aarti, lifting Squidgy from her lap. 'The only clue I have to who I am is this label on my cuddly toy. I found it in a dusty old room where Aunt had thrown it, but I know he's mine. And Aunt gave me the brooch as a gift.'

Beth read the writing under Squidgy's arm:

Lantern Hall, Blackberry Lane, Nottinghamshire

In the morning Aarti sat wrapped in the blanket on the armchair with Skye by her feet and clutched Squidgy tight. She felt so tired she dozed with her eyes half open, her head still thick with sleep. The sound of the sea whooshed in through the open window and the *caw-caw* of the birds came fluttering in behind.

Jim and Beth sat around the table eating breakfast, talking in low voices. She heard them mention Euan's name in a whisper, and more things that she couldn't work out.

Jim touched her softly on the arm. 'Aarti, we need to find your family and let them know you're safe. Do you remember I told you about my cousin, the police officer? We gave him the address from your cuddly toy. But if they don't hear anything by tonight, they'll have to do a TV appeal . . . but let's hope they hear something before then.'

'What's a TV appeal?' asked Aarti.

Jim and Beth exchanged a glance and Beth pointed to the TV attached to the wall. Aarti had read about TVs, of course, but never seen one.

'Best I show you,' Beth said. She picked up a controller and pressed it. Suddenly the room was filled with faces and buzzing loud noise. Aarti pulled the blanket over her head, her heart beating loudly. It was way louder and brighter than she'd ever imagined.

Jim grabbed the controller and quickly turned it off.

She lowered the blanket. 'I've never seen that before,' gasped Aarti.

'Sorry, Aarti, that must have been very frightening,' he said. 'But do you see what we mean? Most people have one of these, so we can put you on the news and send your story all over the world if we need to.'

'We'll find your family and your home,' said Beth, putting an arm round Aarti's shoulders.

Jim stirred a pan of milk on the range and brought Aarti a hot mug of chocolate. 'No more worrying now.'

Aarti watched them both carefully. She liked them and understood a little more what it meant to be cared for, but what was going to happen to her? Fear suddenly snapped into her stomach. She didn't know if she could live in this place with so much noise and so many new things that she didn't understand. And she couldn't go back to the island because nobody knew where it was.

'Hey now,' said Beth, wiping Aarti's tears. 'It's still early. The police are amazing and they'll be contacting each other up and down the country – we just have to give it a bit more time.'

Aarti suddenly remembered the things of Aunt's that she had put in her rucksack. Maybe she should show them to Beth and Jim – there might be a way of uncovering something about Aunt.

She fetched her rucksack from the bedroom and showed them the photos and certificates and letters she had brought from the locked room at the abbey. 'This is Aunt.'

Beth held the yellowing photo of Aunt collecting something from a stage and peered at it.

'She was young then, but when I knew her she was older, quite a lot older than that. And this certificate is hers too.'

'She was a bright woman to get a First in Economics.'

'Can you tell me anything about her?'

'Not much from just these, hen, but we could do some research . . . it doesn't seem right though, even if she did adopt you, that she should take you so far away from anywhere to a place so remote you couldn't see anyone else.'

Aarti touched the brooch. Her feelings for Aunt were so mixed up; Aarti missed her one minute and felt relieved to be away from her the next. And Beth was right: why *had* she taken her so far away?

28

Aarti was in the garden playing with Skye when she heard Jim calling her from the open kitchen door. 'We've got news!'

Fear and excitement whipped through her body as she ran towards Beth and Jim, her heart thrumming under her ribs. Skye thought she was playing a game and leapt up at her as she sprinted along the windy path.

Beth's face was beaming and Jim's eyes were crinkle-kind.

'We've had good news, come inside,' said Beth.

They went into the kitchen and Beth made Aarti sit on the armchair. It felt like insects were crawling in her stomach as she jiggled about impatiently.

'The police in Nottingham went to the address on the label of your toy and – they found your parents.'

Aarti couldn't speak; she felt her hands make tight

fists and she waited for Beth to say more.

Jim put an arm around Aarti. 'The police haven't told us very much, just that your parents are on a plane and they'll be here as soon as they can.'

'We're a fair way from England here,' said Beth, her eyes glistening. 'They won't be here until tomorrow but the police have found them.'

Aarti's voice trembled. 'So it wasn't true what Aunt told me . . . that they were dead and that she adopted me?'

Beth folded Aarti in her arms. 'You poor wee thing.'

Even though the fog of the past was lifting, Aarti still didn't understand why Aunt had taken her away, but it made sense why she hadn't told her anything, that she'd lied to her, and suddenly she felt a flash of anger. 'All those years,' sobbed Aarti, hot tears streaming down her cheeks. 'She made me feel like I didn't matter, she said that nobody wanted me except her . . . but all the time I had parents, people who cared about me.'

Beth stroked her hair. 'They'll be here soon . . . it's all going to be fine.'

'You're a strong lassie,' said Jim. 'You made it away through that storm and everything all by yourself.'

'But why did she take me? Why would she do

that?' Aarti asked.

Beth held her close as she sobbed in mingled happiness, rage and confusion.

Aarti didn't say anything more about Euan. She didn't understand what had happened to him and why he wasn't on the boat when Jim rescued them, but she clasped the shell tight and thought about him and all the things he said and did, like there were two versions of him, the strange Euan and her friend Euan.

Aarti couldn't sleep that night. Excitement buzzed like something magical around her. She kept opening her eyes and hearing the breeze outside, the sea washing against the harbour wall, the creaking of the trees in the garden, until she got out of bed and opened the curtains. She threw the window wide and breathed in the cool night air.

'Euan, wherever you are – thank you,' she whispered. She didn't know if she was just imagining it, but she heard his flute playing the tune out across the water.

She watched the sea darkened by the night, white-tipped waves ruffling in on the tide, and she couldn't believe that at last she knew she had a family and was going to meet them.

She held Squidgy tight, breathed in his smell. The rose scent that clung to his fur seemed to be stronger tonight. When she went back to bed she felt a stillness at last and fell into a deep sleep, lulled by the rhythm of the sea.

When daylight came to wake her, she flicked open her eyes. She had never felt like this before. A huge gigantic something was about to happen and even though she didn't know exactly what it would be like, she knew it was going to be good.

She quietly went to the bathroom. It was strange seeing herself in the mirror: her face with its smooth golden skin, a scattering of freckles across the ridge of her nose, her eyes as brown as a hazelnut and the tiny birthmark at the tip of her left eyebrow. She splashed her cheeks with water and dabbed on the face cream that Beth had given her, combed out her hair, long down to her waist, crinkled from the plait.

Would she look like her parents? Would they know straight away that it was her and that she belonged to them?

Aarti slipped back to the bedroom and changed into the clothes that Beth had put on the chair last night. She had said she was sorry that they didn't have many shops up here and there was no time to go to the closest town either, so this outfit meant for her granddaughter would have to do. She stepped into the red-and-white spotted dress and buttoned it up at the front, put on the bright white ankle socks with the wavy fringe of red, and finally the striped pumps.

Aarti looked at herself in the long mirror and wriggled. Who was this girl looking back at her?

A door slammed outside and she hurried to the open window, ducked down and peered out to the road in front of the cottage. A taxi had just pulled up, and a man and woman got out and crunched their way down the gravel path.

Aarti's heart fluttered, her hands trembled, as she walked to the top of the stairs and peeped down to the front door.

Beth was already there, and she turned the handle and let them in.

29

'Come in, come in,' tinkled Beth's voice as Aarti's parents stepped into the square hallway of the cottage.

Aarti saw her mum's quick brown eyes dart up the stairs, reach out to her straight away, and in that moment all the years of tangled memories began to unravel. She rushed up, grasped Aarti in her arms and pulled her close.

Aarti couldn't help it, she wanted to tuck in like a baby bird, but she felt herself stiffen and stood awkwardly, uncomfortably, against her mum.

The faint rose scent that had been buried in Squidgy's fur hit Aarti's nose now like the most beautiful smell in the world. It was warm and comforting and as wonderful as waking up to summer after years of rainy days. At last she could see the face that was blank in her dreams.

'My baby,' her mother breathed into Aarti's hair.

At last, Aarti let herself lean into her mum's body. 'Mama,' she wept, allowing all the hurt free. She could hear her sobs turn to wails and she let everything out, her breath beating rhythmically from deep within her, tender beneath her ribs.

Her mum held her firm, pulled her closer as her cries eventually faded and only the breaths remained. Aarti sensed the imprints of her familiar hands upon her and deep down she knew she was home, at last.

When her mum finally released her, she took Aarti's face between her palms and searched every inch, touched her reddened cheeks, traced the freckles on her nose and the tiny birthmark at the very edge of her left eyebrow and kissed them all better.

'Eight years, Aarti,' she sobbed. 'We never stopped searching, we never stopped hoping . . . my beautiful baby, my beautiful girl.' She took Aarti's hand and led her down the stairs where her dad lifted Aarti high in the air, whispered in her ear, 'Chand – we found you.'

Aarti couldn't find her words, but the name jolted back clouds of memories, of her magical fox and the island, as her feet touched the ground again.

'This is Police Sergeant Sutherland,' said Jim as they went into the kitchen. 'Remember I told you about him? He's my cousin and is here to check that everything is as it should be.'

Sergeant Sutherland looked over at some papers and passports that Aarti's parents showed him and he nodded before handing them back. 'I'll be off then, I'll see myself out.'

'Thanks, Arran,' said Jim. 'We'll see you soon.'

Beth and Jim offered cups of tea and sandwiches and Skye sat by Aarti's feet. Everyone was chattering and a glow of happiness hung over the snug kitchen as Aarti sneaked a piece of ham from her sandwich and slipped it to Skye.

'Hey,' said Jim. 'You'll have yourself a friend for life there if you keep feeding him treats.'

'Thank you so much,' said Aarti's mum, hugging Beth and Jim. 'You've made us so happy, you brought our baby back.'

Beth swiped at her cheeks and hugged her back. 'Keep in touch, won't you? Let us know how she settles.'

'Thank you for looking after me,' croaked Aarti, her throat sore and scratched.

Jim ruffled her hair. 'Come back and see us whenever you want.'

'Look at you, in that dress.' Beth touched her cheek. 'Here's your rucksack with your things and that toy of yours.'

Aarti looked at the seahorse brooch on Squidgy's chest and unpinned it. 'I want you to have this. I think it's worth something – maybe you can use it for the sea rescue fund to keep more people safe.'

'Are you sure?' asked Jim.

'Aunt gave it to me, but I want you to have it. I want it to do some good. And I think . . . I think I need to let go of it. And of Aunt too.' Aarti wrapped her arms around Beth, and Skye poked his muzzle between them. She gave him a big cuddle. At last she felt safe, even though there were still so many questions about what had happened, about the woman who called herself her aunt.

The journey home to Lantern Hall was a long one, involving a taxi, a train, a hotel stay overnight, and finally, in the morning, a plane. Aarti was astounded and afraid, the feeling of flying in the clouds unreal. She gripped the armrests, trying to swallow her fear.

Eventually Aarti told her parents all about the island and all about Aunt and what had happened to her. She told them about Chand and how she had rescued Euan, and how together they had left the island. Her parents, one on either side, comforted her, but she still couldn't get used to being touched and sat straight as an arrow with her fists scrunched in her lap.

They told her how they used to call her Chand, their moon, about her brother Amman who was two years older than her and had missed her so much.

Aarti felt her stomach twist. Maybe that's why the name Chand had seemed so right when she had found her dear little fox with the crescent moon between his eyes. Now she knew that even though things had been so bad with Aunt, she was safe and what had happened was wrong. When she asked her parents why Aunt had done what she'd done, sitting between them on the roaring plane, her parents had shared a glance before her mum started to speak carefully.

'The truth is, the police don't know. I don't think we'll ever truly know. But . . . it seems to me that she was a very lonely woman who desperately wanted a child to pour her love into.'

Aarti felt her eyes sting. Aunt had loved her, in her way – she knew that. But Aarti was angry, now. She didn't know if she could ever forgive Aunt for everything she had stolen from Aarti by stealing her from her family. 'I wasn't hers to take,' she said, her voice thick with tears.

'You weren't,' said her dad, squeezing Aarti's hand.

'She should never have taken you. But what matters is you're back with us now. And we all get to start again.'

When at last they landed at the airport, her mum kept Aarti pressed close to her side like she was afraid she might disappear in a puff of smoke, and Aarti was slowly letting herself relax. Her mum kept fiddling with Aarti's hair and smoothing her arm. 'We missed you so much.'

'Let's get you home,' said her dad, as they stepped into a taxi and drove the final stretch along busy roads and smaller country lanes surrounded by fields.

Aarti was sleepy and exhausted. She leant against her dad's arm, felt the comfort of his scratchy jacket as they turned into a narrow road and she read *Blackberry Lane* on the sign, the same as Squidgy Rabbit's label. Her heart beat more quickly when the car continued along a wide driveway, through tall iron gates with the name *Lantern Hall* in cut-out ironwork across the top.

The memories whooshed over her like a breeze from the past. The sound of the car crunching on gravel, the chitter-chatter of birdsong, the soft scent of flowers and cut grass, and the voice calling her name, 'Aarti . . . where are you?'

And then she remembered playing in this garden, hiding from her brother, running away from him too far so he wouldn't find her . . .

The car came to a stop in front of a whitewashed double-fronted house surrounded by rambling gardens, trees dotted higgledy-piggledy and, beyond the garden, fields of newly planted green wheat.

They got out of the taxi and it drove off down the drive. The sun sparkled over them like it was welcoming Aarti home and the wind whispered through the trees. She stood in the porch, breathing in all the scents of her home and they prickled at the corners of her mind, lifting thoughts that she couldn't yet speak.

At the window she saw a face peep through the shutters.

'That's your brother Amman – he's been so excited to see you again!'

30

Aarti stepped through the front door, nerves and excitement zigzagging from her belly and fluttering under her ribs. Her dad squeezed her shoulder, slipped his hand gently into Aarti's and led her into the hallway. Her pumps padded softly on the old wooden floor and her eyes darted about the grand house: the high ceiling edged with fancy plasterwork, the sweeping stairs in the centre of the hall, and all the open doors on either side, sunshine spooling from the rooms.

In one of the doorways she spotted the same brown eyes that had been peeping through the shutters. Her brother Amman sidled out of the room, looked from Aarti to the floor and back again. He didn't say anything, just gave a lopsided smile and fiddled with his nails.

Their mum put her arms around both their

shoulders and brought them together. 'I think he wants to say welcome home, Aarti.'

Her dad joined the circle and pulled everyone tight. 'Home at last,' he said, tears creeping into the corners of his eyes.

'You two get lunch,' said her mum. 'I'll show Aarti to her room.'

They went up the carpeted staircase, Aarti sliding her hand along the smooth wooden bannister, looking about her at the large paintings splashed with colour that hung on the landing.

'This is your room – do you remember?'

Aarti clutched Squidgy and stepped in. Along one wall were framed paintings and she slowly studied them: a black-and-red bird, a bunch of yellow flowers with *Happy Mother's Day* in careful first writing, and a letter to Father Christmas with a wish list.

'Did I paint these?'

'Yes . . . just take your time, Aarti.'

From the shelf above the cosy bed her mum picked up a small tin and opened it. 'Your first lock of baby hair.'

Even though Aarti couldn't remember everything, by looking at her things and hearing what her mum was telling her, scraps of images and feelings were popping into her head and beginning to slot into place.

Her mum opened the doors of the whitewashed wardrobes that took up a whole wall. There were hanging rails with clothes for a much smaller Aarti, jumpers and dresses and a few bigger things. Aarti put her rucksack by the bed.

'We can go shopping or order some things online – you can choose. I had these sent quickly, when I got the call from Beth and Jim.' She picked out some leggings and a pretty shirt. 'Have a bath and get changed.'

Aarti pushed open a door into a small, neat bathroom. Her mum twisted the taps and began to run hot, steamy water. She dribbled some bubbles in and the whole room smelt of flowers.

When Aarti took off the dress she saw her mum studying the bruises and scratches on her arms and legs. Her mum opened the mirrored cabinet, took a jar of ointment and dabbed the balm gently where it was needed.

'I had to do lots of outdoor jobs, like chopping firewood, collecting berries and fishing. But I loved being in the wilderness of the island. It looked after me and protected me.'

'We need to find out about this woman, who she was and what happened. We've given everything we know to the police already and they'll want to talk to you – if it's OK with you, Aarti? And you don't have to think about it now, but we'll find a doctor, someone who will help you to understand what happened.'

Aarti got into the warm bath and let the water relax her. It was hard to imagine that she wouldn't ever need to walk out across cold snow in bare feet, or do hours of ballet practice, wake in the middle of an icy night and go fishing. She was home with the people who loved her.

'I'll go and help the boys with the food – come down when you're ready.'

After the bath she dressed in the leggings and shirt her mum had laid out on the bed. The outfit felt strange after all the years of wearing musty old clothes, and she pressed her nose to the shirt, its fresh smell bringing a smile to her face. She tucked Squidgy into her bed where he belonged.

But her thoughts kept returning to Euan and it filled her with sadness. He had been such a good friend. From the rucksack she took out the story they'd made together on that rainy day at the abbey and she traced the figures he had painted: Krishna, Amergin and the blue gods, and the Awen symbol in the corner. And she remembered the confusing things he'd said during the storm, when his face turned strange and he became the *other* Euan.

A call from downstairs jolted her from her thoughts and she spread their story on her desk and ran down to join her family. They were sitting around a big table, doors open to the garden. She slipped in beside her brother, who took a big scoopful of strawberry puree and drizzled it on to Aarti's pancakes.

He'd made a card and pushed it towards her. 'Welcome back.' The card had a big smiley face on it, and along the bottom he'd written Aarti's name.

'Thank you,' said Aarti, placing the card by her plate. She gave him a smile. So this was her brother – someone who made her a card and made sure she had enough on her plate. She was ravenous and stuffed the pancakes into her mouth.

After they had finished, Aarti and Amman went into the garden. Now that they were alone he seemed unsure of himself and dragged behind, kicking at the grass, tugging at the sleeves of his sweatshirt.

'What is it?' asked Aarti, stepping closer to him.

He shuffled away and Aarti swallowed the lump that had crept into her throat.

He flicked a glance back towards the house before turning to Aarti. 'All Mum and Dad ever talked about was you,' he blurted.

His comment startled her. 'W . . . what do you mean?'

Amman's cheeks glowed red. 'I mean, maybe now you're back, they'll start to notice me.'

They both stayed quiet, staring everywhere but at each other.

'And I know they've never said they blame me – but I was the last person to see you on that day.'

Aarti frowned. 'Of course they don't blame you.' Anger suddenly pounded at her temples. 'You can't begin to imagine what it was like, Amman.' Hot tears sprang across her cheeks.

31

'I'm sorry,' said Amman, looping his arm around Aarti's shoulder. 'I didn't mean to make you cry, it's just one minute you were here and the next I couldn't find you.'

Aarti brushed the tears with the back of her hand. 'I . . . I remember playing a game with you.'

'Hide and seek,' he said. 'We were only little – you were four and I was six.'

'And I wanted to hide somewhere you wouldn't find me.'

'I was counting and when I got to a hundred I went all around the garden but I couldn't see you anywhere.'

They walked to the edge of the garden together, to the side which had a small lane running alongside it.

'Aarti, it *was* my fault.'

'It wasn't your fault. We were just playing a game.'

Aarti bobbed down low and crawled into a hollow in the hedge. 'I knew you wouldn't find me here, but I waited and waited and got bored.' The memory was bouncing back as she smelt the green leaves and brushed against the twiggy branches. 'So I went out the other end and walked along the lane. And that's when I met a woman – Aunt. She . . . she asked me my name and what I was doing, and I told her I was trying to hide from you, with Squidgy Rabbit. She said she had a really good hiding place and did I want to see.' Aarti felt her heart pumping. 'So I went with her and she took me away.'

'I'm so sorry, Aarti.' He wiped his eyes. 'It must have been so horrible. And then I had to tell Mum that I couldn't find you and she had told me to always look after you and I didn't.'

Aarti held her brother's hand. 'It's OK. It's not your fault . . . and I'm here now. I had a little friend on the island, a fox that I called Chand.'

'Like Mum and Dad's name for you?'

'He had a white mark like a crescent moon on his forehead and he was always there when I needed him.'

They went back into the garden and sat on the grass. Aarti told him more about the island and about her life there with Aunt and how she'd found

Euan washed up on the beach. He was impressed with all the things she could do like sailing a boat, climbing cliffs and swimming in waterfalls.

'The really strange thing is, though,' she continued, 'there's something about Euan that I can't explain . . . I don't understand why he wasn't on the boat when they rescued us. I could see him plain as anything – but the crew said there was nobody there.' She touched the shell necklace. 'He gave me this.'

'We could put his name into the computer and see what we find.'

'What do you mean, "computer"? There are some things that I've never seen before, or at least don't really remember. Like TV at Beth and Jim's house – that was so loud and frightening.'

'It's like a TV, a bit anyway – but it's to find information, so maybe we can find some information about your friend Euan. What was his second name?'

'He was Euan Macleod.'

'Come on, we can use the computer in the study.'

They rushed in, nearly knocking their dad over. 'Glad you're getting to know each other again.'

'In here.' Amman went into one of the other rooms off the hallway. It was lined with bookshelves and posters of their mum playing the flute.

'Euan played the flute as well,' said Aarti, staring up at the poster.

'Mum's a well-known classical Indian flautist. She used to travel all over the world, but since . . . you know, you disappeared she only plays in the UK and then not very often.' Amman pinged on the computer.

Aarti pulled up a chair next to Amman and peered at the screen as it lit up and he began typing Euan's name in.

A whole list of Euan Macleods came up in rows.

'Mmm . . . how old was he?'

'About my age – at least that's what he looked like.'

'About eleven or twelve then?'

'Yeah, I guess.'

Amman typed in again, adding the age range.

'He had a boat called the *Dunter* and lived on the coast somewhere in Scotland.'

Amman typed all these things in, and this time Aarti's face flashed with shock. 'That's him!'

'But Aarti, how can it be? This boy drowned in a sailing accident. It says his boat *Dunter* was washed up.'

Aarti read the article on the screen. 'But look, it says they never found him . . . he washed up on the island and I nursed him back to health.'

Aarti stared at the photo of her friend looking back at her. His smiley freckled face, his eyes dark as a winter's night. Next to him, his ma with her black hair swept back by the wind, wearing a silver pendant with the Awen symbol on it, his wee sister Mhairi holding on to him round the waist, and his da with his arm flung around Euan's shoulder.

What happened to you, Euan? Aarti felt her throat tighten.

'Aarti, look at the date. This happened eight years ago in early March – that was when you disappeared, on that exact date.' He touched her arm. 'Don't get upset . . . do you want me to print his photo off for you?'

Aarti nodded; she couldn't speak. None of this made any sense and she suddenly felt so tired. The photo appeared from the printer and Aarti held it tenderly in her hands. 'Thank you, Amman.'

She went to her room and put the photo on her desk beside the story she and Euan had made together. She remembered all the strange things about Euan that were so hard to explain. How in the low glimmer his face had seemed to change and she had seen spirals like ink tattoos across his face and body on the night she had pulled him from the water. She recalled what she had seen when she followed him to the beach that night, and her surprise when he found the Awen symbol carved behind the wall of the shrine that she'd never noticed before, his confusion over the flute around his neck that he only seemed to play at night.

Exhausted, she collapsed on her bed, and even though it was still daytime, she slipped on her pyjamas and got into the warm bed, pulled the duvet around her and closed her eyes.

Somehow Euan had heard her calling. On the boat he had tried to explain how he had heard her cries. The stories in the Krishna book talked about how Krishna was born in a prison and then magically transported away. They talked about spirits, like wisps of air that could move in ways not possible for humans . . . Maybe Euan was all these things.

She hadn't thought about it before, but Euan had appeared only a couple of days after Chand disappeared. Almost as if Chand had been watching over her and then Euan had taken his place. She'd always felt the island was looking after her – perhaps Chand and Euan had been part of that. Perhaps they'd even been one and the same.

Euan had said on the boat that they had saved each other – she hoped that was true. Perhaps now he could rest in peace.

That night, she drifted to sleep listening to the new sounds of her home: the low chatter of her parents and Amman still eating supper, faint music tinkling up the stairs, the *glug glug* of water shooting through the pipes and the noises outside that were so different to what she was used to. No thundering rain cascading on the roof and dripping on to her face while she was sleeping, no shushing of the sea as it threw high waves at the rocks, and no shuddering of the wind as it whistled through the woods.

32

It was still dark when Aarti was woken by a sound outside her window. It was like a barking she knew so well. She slipped from her bed, tiptoed across the room and pushed open the curtains.

The night was still and stars shone over the field beyond the garden. In the ebony night the moon rose swollen and pale, wobbling between the clouds. She peered into the night and at first couldn't see anything, but when she strained her eyes, squinting to see better, she saw the outline of a fox, sliding low to the ground.

Aarti slung on a jumper and quickly left the room, tripped silently down the stairs and into the breakfast room. Unlocking the doors to the garden, she stepped on to the damp grass. The sharp scent of fox clung to the air and wafted its way to Aarti's nose. She crouched down and held out her palm. If only she had some walnuts. She knew foxes liked walnuts.

Her heart beat fiercely as she enticed the fox to her, making clicking sounds with her tongue. *Could it be Chand come all this way to find me?*

The fox sniffed the ground, lifted his head towards Aarti and cautiously began trotting in her direction.

'There,' she breathed, letting him sniff her outstretched hand. Her heart gave a patter, as for a moment she thought she saw a white curve on his forehead – but it was only her imagination and the darkness of the night playing tricks on her.

She let a small tear trickle down her nose. 'Do you know Chand? He was my friend and I loved him.'

An owl hooted out across the field. 'Oooweee,' it screeched. 'Ooowee.' The fox tossed his head, sniffed the air and disappeared further into the garden. Aarti watched his tail as he swished it behind him until she couldn't see him any more.

She went back into the house, closed the doors and returned to her room. It was hard not to miss Chand, but maybe this fox would come back again and she could make friends with him.

In the morning sunbeams spun through the window, glittering and bouncing from the walls, spilling on to

Aarti's sleeping face. Already, her weather-worn skin was turning smooth and her cheekbones were losing their sharpness and the line of dirt that ringed her neck like a piece of lace was nearly gone.

As she slept, she breathed away Aunt's stain from her, but took the sacred parts of the island and tucked them safely away, in the tender spot beneath her ribs where she would guard them like jewels.

Later, Amman knocked on the door and let himself in. 'I've brought you some hot chocolate.'

He put it on the bedside table and Aarti woke blearily, rubbing at the sleep in her eyes. She sat up, clasped her hands around the mug and blew at the snowy white cream on top.

'Friends?' asked Amman.

'Friends,' replied Aarti.

The sound of flute music travelled up the stairs. 'Mum's practising loads now. She said that maybe we'll all go to India this year. She can play some concerts and we can all stay with family.'

Aarti swallowed. 'I know you're going to think this is crazy after what we found out about Euan yesterday, but when I found him on the beach he had a flute around his neck, and eventually sometimes – at night – he played it, and the tune he played was this sort of music, Indian music.'

Amman didn't say anything, not that he thought Aarti needed more sleep or that she was imagining things again or to stop being silly – nothing. He just listened.

The playing got louder and closer to Aarti and her mum came in playing the beautiful lilting music. She carried on playing, gently filling the room with the soulful sounds that spoke of dusty hot roads, black-and-amber striped tigers hiding in lush green jungles and a whole other world that also belonged to Aarti.

Her mum took the flute from her lips. 'This is the tune I used to play to you both when you were little. Amman used to use an upside-down saucepan and would bang away on it and you used to dance around the room, twirling and twirling until you were dizzy.'

'I sort of remember it,' said Aarti, lifting the memory of herself from a darkened buried place.

'You loved it. You used to twist your chubby little hands like the classical dancers and I even brought you some ghungroos back from a tour I did in India. You used to tie them round your ankles,' she giggled, 'and the bells would drive us nuts.'

'Food,' called Aarti's dad from the breakfast room.

'Your dad's been busy making aloo paratha – it's our typical lazy Sunday breakfast.'

'And spiced Indian tea,' said Amman, 'with plenty of sugar.'

'I can't remember them, but I think as soon as I take a bite all my taste memories will come flooding back.'

Together they went downstairs and joined her dad in the sunny breakfast room. He was busy by the stove, turning the paratha, engulfed by clouds of burnt buttery smoke that floated out of the open doors.

'Hey, guys – hope you're all hungry.'

Aarti noticed her mum rest a watchful eye on her, and returned a smile that told her that she was OK. She was strong, and despite everything that had happened she was finding out who she was, one slow step at a time.

One
year
later

33

A year passed and slowly Aarti threw herself into life with her family. All the things that had drifted like wisps of shady memories the whole time she was on the island became real. She went to secondary school and made friends, had sleepovers where her mum tried so hard to make things perfect for her, and she found that the thing she loved more than anything was to write.

She loved being outdoors, and when they went on family camping trips, they were all so impressed with how she lit a fire, set up the tent and caught more mackerel than any of them.

But during the quiet moments when Aarti was falling asleep, or watching a murmuration of starlings, or staring up at the vast dark sky speckled with stars like gemstones, that's when the island rushed to fill her body and when she thought of Euan and what had happened.

Aarti's mum and dad kept in touch with Beth and Jim, as they'd said they would. Aarti had made Jim promise that if he ever came across a beautiful island with a tumbledown abbey and standing stones above the harbour, with a mountain peak rising out of the swirls of mist, where nobody lived but golden eagles, seabirds and puffins, that he had to let her know – it was *her* island and she had the papers to prove it.

And one day a letter, addressed to Aarti, dropped on the doormat. The letter from Beth and Jim explained that on a recent fishing trip Jim and the crew had sailed close by an island that fitted Aarti's description. It was a long way off from anywhere and was just as she had described.

The Scottish village of Arisaig was a long way from Nottinghamshire, and like her parents had done a year ago, this time the family took a plane, a train and finally a taxi to get there. Aarti stepped from the car to the cries of the seabirds gathering over the dancing waves in front of Beth and Jim's little cottage, the white sands beautiful against the deep-blue sea. The curtains twitched and the door flung open.

Beth rushed down the path to greet them with Jim

following close behind. They folded Aarti into a hug and made a fuss of her.

'Look how tall you are,' said Beth. 'Nearly catching up with your brother here.'

'So lovely to see you both again,' said Mum. 'This is Amman.' She darted her eyes around, like she was wondering what this trip would unlock and if she was ready for it.

'I have a wee surprise for you,' said Jim. 'After the incident last summer and the article in the paper, your friend Euan's family were in touch.'

Aarti felt her chest tighten.

'If it's OK with you, they'd like to join us on the trip. I – thought you might like it.'

Aarti wasn't sure. What would they think about what happened? But it might make it easier for them, even though it was still so difficult to explain. 'Yes, sure.'

They made their way to the harbour where Jim's fishing boat was tugging against the waves. Aarti recognized Euan's family straight away. They were huddled together, looking out to sea.

Euan's ma turned as they arrived. She held her arms out to Aarti and tears slipped down her cheek.

Aarti took her hand and gave it a squeeze. 'Euan told me all about you.'

Aarti was shocked that Mhairi had grown, but of course she was older than Aarti, even though when Euan talked about her, she was only six – what did she expect? That even though, as the papers said, it was eight years since Euan drowned, she would not have grown up?

'I know all of this is going to seem crazy to you,' began Aarti. 'But – but I saw Euan as clearly as I see you now.'

'His spirit came to save you,' said Euan's ma, touching her Awen pendant. 'And now he can rest in peace.'

Euan's da looked at the ground and then out to sea. Aarti could see Euan's eyes in his da's face, just as he had told her, and it made her feel like she already knew him.

'He told me how much he loved you, how much he missed you all. He said you'd be knitting a scarf most likely . . . while you waited.'

Euan's ma touched the sea-green scarf bulging from her bag. 'It's pretty long.' She smiled. 'It was for him.'

'Come on,' said Jim. 'We can talk more once we're on our way.'

Everyone piled into the boat and once Beth had put the kettle on in the small cabin and Euan's ma brought out some home-made tablet, the nerves that spun between them slipped away like salt water. Euan was right, his ma's crunchy tablet was the best.

For two days they journeyed away from Arisaig into the vast emerald sea, followed by gannets and fulmars enticed by the scent of fish which clung to the boat. Aarti told Euan's family what had happened, from the night she found him, to how he'd disappeared on the boat. His da brushed his cheek, said he was always drawn to the sea and was such a good sailor but should never have gone out alone.

On the first evening, as the stars popped into the sky all of a sudden, while they sipped hot chocolate out on the deck, his ma eventually sang the lullaby about the blue gods and told funny stories about Euan as a baby. They thanked Aarti, because at least now they knew more about what had happened.

Late on the second day, as fine mist rose off the sea, far away in the distance a smudge appeared on the horizon. Aarti swallowed. Was she ready for this? Coming back was going to bring all those memories of the hard years back, but the doctor said it was a good idea and it was important to face the past. And the island belonged to her.

Amman put his arm around his sister and Mhairi

came to join them at the front of the boat. Her green eyes sparked in the sunlight. 'You're really brave doing this . . . and thank you for letting us come.'

Jim guided the boat closer to the island and it rose from the sea, bathed in the golden sun, wrapped in summer beauty, like a living breathing creature.

Aarti's stomach turned a flip as the peak of the mountain came into view, and gradually all the things that were familiar to her: the curve of white sand on the harbour, the stones standing guard above the beach.

'Look,' she cried, when the chimney stacks came into view. 'There's smoke.'

'It's only a cloud, Aarti,' said her mum, holding tightly to her hand.

And as the boat glided through the shallow waters, Aarti saw the thing she most missed. At the water's edge, with his rust-red paws dipped into the sea, was her fox Chand, the crescent moon between his eyes glimmering in the clear early morning.

'Mama, look! It's my Chand, come back to me.'

As the boat came in closer, Aarti gasped. 'Foot-prints!' Her eyes followed the line of prints, and where they stopped she saw Euan, his freckled face smiling at her.

'Euan!' she called.

But in the next moment he faded, and all she could see was Chand, and the new moon as it peeped out from behind the standing stones.

LETTER FROM THE AUTHOR

I have family connections to Scotland and love the Scottish islands, so when I began thinking about writing book three, there were a few wishes I had for the story. I wanted to set it on a wild Scottish island and share my love with readers, I wanted Aarti to have a fox friend and I was also curious to see whether there were any links between Eastern and Western mythologies that I could weave into the story. As often happens to me when I begin to go down rabbit holes, I found some surprising connections. Did you know that the Druids had a lot in common with the ancient Brahmins? The Druids are thought to have walked thousands of miles, travelling all the way to Tibet. The Brahmins and the Druids shared knowledge with each other and they both had a similar structure of profession and learning. But their strongest connection was the power of nature and it was this that I wanted to keep at the heart of my story.

'Aarti' means the ritual of lighting a flame and sending a prayer – even though Aarti has to search hard for answers about who she is, it is the discovery of a natural magic inside herself that, in the end, leads her home.

One of the things we love as a family is travelling, and we have spent many happy times on pristine Scottish beaches munching on tablet, which I managed to sneak into the story – so don't forget to find some next time you're in Scotland. It's delicious!

ACKNOWLEDGEMENTS

Bringing a book from its first idea to the thing you can hold lightly in your hands, open and devour is a feat that needs an army behind it. And so, I start my thanks . . . It always begins with family because without them it would simply be impossible. Thank you, then, to the person who is in my thoughts every day, my dearest grandmother Chinty Kaur Bains. It's incredible how powerful our early connections to unconditional love are. She made me believe that I *could* even when I didn't know what it was that I wanted to do. To my wonderful mum, who amazes me with her enthusiasm and love, to my husband Ian who has been my greatest flag-waver and without whose support none of this would have been possible. To my sons Gem and Satchen, who have witnessed how long things can take and have grown in the blink of an eye into amazing young men. To my siblings, Balraj, Sherry, Randhiraj, Dip and Amolack, who have showered me with support and have been so proud – it has meant so much! To the next generation of the Bilan family: Avarni, Jyodh, Arran, Ashari, Rajan, Xanthe, Tara, Rubuen, Rani, Evan, Jadan, Arron and Aneve. To my dear Judy, who I know would have been so chuffed.

It's been a tough year – the challenges of Covid have meant no outings to Chicken House HQ to drink tea and munch cake, or to hear first-hand what needed tightening, stripping out, embellishing. But the team have been there behind a Zoom screen, in PJs (shhh . . .) and hats, with virtual mugs of tea, making everything go smoothly. So hugest thanks to Barry Cunningham for his star suggestion! To my dream editor Kesia, who understands what I'm aiming for even when I'm not sure myself, and for asking just the right questions to bring on the perfect balance of magic. To the wonderful Rachel Leyshon for her very welcome eagle eye. Rachel Hickman made my dreams come true when she said 'yes' to flaps, 'yes' to a map and 'yes' to the most magically stunning cover I could have hoped for. To Margaux Carpentier and Steve Wells for the beautiful cover and Alexis Snell for the divine map. Thank you Jazz for everything this year. To Laura, Esther and Sarah for sprinkling stardust and magicking a book from my typed pages. And to the amazing Elinor Bagenal for spreading the story love.

A million thanks to my agent Ben for believing in Aarti and for always bringing a fresh eye to the table, as well as flowers.

Thank you to the super-talented Carolyn Rayner who manages to turn my ideas into the most gorgeously arty offerings for everything web-based. To Belinda Borries for all her expert advice on mental health and psychology.

When I began my writing journey way back on the MA WYP Bath Spa, one of its gifts was the support of fellow writers and friends. Mel and Miranda are the constants, always on hand to help with ideas, drafts and thoughts – thank you! I have the champagne ready!

To the staff and pupils at my Patron of Reading school (my old school), the ever-impressive Mellers Primary in Nottingham, the best school ever! Thank you to my new Year Six 'fans' for helping me to finally decide on the name *Aarti & the Blue Gods* for this, my third book! Good taste, guys! You will be moving up in September, but always remember your dreams and what you want to achieve – you will all be reaching for the stars!

It has been such an honour to be part of Nottingham City of Literature – thank you for all the opportunities, and when I step inside the beautiful new library, I will raise a glass and recall the first time I went to my local Nottingham library as a small girl, so excited by all the stories waiting to be discovered!

To the wonderful MA Creative Writing for Young People course at Bath Spa University. Especially to Dr Lucy Christopher for inviting me to open their guest lectures this year, and for all their continuing support.

Thank you to all the teachers, librarians, booksellers and reviewers for going on adventures with me and sharing my stories with children. Special thanks to: Lauren St John, Sita Brahmachari, Scott Evans, Katherine Rundell, Piers Torday, Kiran Millwood Hargrave, Jessie Burton, Bali Rai and Frank Cottrell-Boyce for your kindness, generosity and support. And finally, to you my readers, whom I can't wait to take on more adventures . . . Where shall we go next?